F ARIDA KARODIA was bor
South Africa which was
novel *Daughters of the Twili*
1969 having previously taug
In Canada she has worked in a variety of jobs, including
teaching, and has written several radio dramas for C.B.C.
She is now a full-time writer.

Daughters of the Twilight was published in 1986 and was a
runner-up in the Fawcett Prize. *Coming Home and Other Stories*
is Farida Karodia's first short story collection. She is
currently working on a second novel.

FARIDA KARODIA

COMING HOME
AND OTHER STORIES

HEINEMANN

Heinemann International
A division of Heinemann Educational Books Ltd
Halley Court, Jordan Hill, Oxford OX2 8EJ

Heinemann Educational Books (Nigeria) Ltd
PMB 5205, Ibadan
Heinemann Kenya Ltd
Kijabe Street, PO Box 45314, Nairobi
Heinemann Educational Boleswa
PO Box 10103, Village Post Office, Gaborone, Botswana
Heinemann Educational Books Inc
70 Court Street, Portsmouth, New Hampshire, 03801, USA
Heinemann Educational Books (Caribbean) Ltd
175 Mountain View Avenue, Kingston 6, Jamaica

LONDON   EDINBURGH   MELBOURNE   SYDNEY
AUCKLAND   SINGAPORE   MADRID

British Library Cataloguing in Publication Data

Karodia, Farida
Coming home and other stories.
I. Title
823[F]   PR9369.3.K3

ISBN 0-435-90738-7
ISBN 0-435-90739-5 export

Typeset by Activity Limited, Salisbury, Wiltshire, England

Printed in Great Britain by
Cox & Wyman Ltd, Reading, Berkshire

CONTENTS

For my daughter Anesia

'... Because I love this soil, this land with its people, as the eye loves the light, as a flute loves the last bit of darkness before dawn when the morning breeze stirs the tops of the trees and the shrubs and the grass with a primordial warm hand. Because I believe in the future of this land ...'

A Season in Paradise by Breyten Breytenbach

Author's Note

I have taken the liberty of changing place names, the names of townships and settings; adding to the existing ones and altering them to my design in order to place the characters and situations in their appropriate surroundings. The characters in this book are all fictitious and are not based on any known person, living or dead.

African terms italicised in the text can be found in the glossary on page 183.

COMING HOME

ONE

I tapped the dottle from my pipe, idly gazing down into the valley where the vines criss-crossed the floor like lattice-work. There was a quality of peace about this scene which was conducive to quiet reflection. At times when I sat here absorbed in the view, I was almost inclined to forget why I had left in the first place.

Whenever my wife, Celia, accompanied me to the farm, she too came out here to sit on the rock which jutted from the hill overlooking the valley. I remember her conjecturing once that Andries van der Merwe's ancestors might have stood on this very spot (where the valley seemed to form a triangle), when they named the farm *Driehoek*.

But at this time of year a feeling of utter desolation settles over, the valley and with the harvest over, the vines await another season's abundance. In the distance the shroud of stillness is shattered by the loud carping of crows as they circle in the heavy air.

I watched Kenny clambering up the rutted footpath to the very top of the hill. Gimpie, the dog, following close on his heels, stopped to examine a rabbit-hole.

'Hey Gimpie!' Kenny called, giving a piercing whistle.

The dog lifted its head, directed a baleful glance at Kenny's voice, and returned to its preoccupation with the hole.

'Gimpie! Gimpie!'

The dog barked and with its nose to the ground, zigzagged through the stunted brown grass.

'Gimpie!' Kenny shouted sternly.

1

With an uneven gait the dog limped across the field towards Kenny's voice. He was a medium-sized dog of no recognisable breed with a fawn coat and large white paws. He was about five years old now, having come to us as a pup after his owner, Kerel Carelse, died. His left front leg was shorter than the rest (the result of being caught in a rabbit trap). At the base of the rock he sniffed the ground, circled four or five times, squatted with his four paws close together and left a dump.

Funny how things change, I mused. After all these years away from the place, it seems that I've actually developed a fondness for the valley with its steamy days and early morning mists. I'm still not at all keen about winter with its cloying, turbulent masses of dark, grey clouds which shut out the sun. At times in winter the thunder echoed from great distances, rumbling and growling on the heels of jagged forks which rent the sky. Other times it came without pause, booming like cannon-shot as it ricocheted off the mountains.

I was reminded of how, as a child, I hated the confinement of this valley, hated the life, the struggle, the rain and the mud; but above all, how I hated my father. Now, after having spent eighteen years in jail for assaulting a white man, he was coming home. And in spite of all the misery he had brought us, Mama's eyes still lit up with expectation each time there was a strange sound outside.

For three generations my family had worked here at *Driehoek*: planting, picking, carrying, and spraying the precious grapes which grew in the fertile valleys of the Boland in the western Cape. Although there was nothing left here for us any more, Mama stayed on, living on a small plot of land she could never own.

'It's too late for me to change my habits,' Mama told me when I asked her to come and stay with us. 'I just want to live out the rest of my life in the arms of this valley.'

Thanks to her I had left *Driehoek* when I was fourteen, and so my children had something other than the valley to look forward to. Although my departure had emancipated me from

2

an existence that had enslaved my ancestors, something always seemed to draw me back here.

I watched Kenny flinging pebbles into the valley and felt a surge of paternal pride that he had grown into a fine boy. I remembered standing on that same spot when I was his age, day-dreaming about voyages of adventure to distant places like those related by Johnny Moses when he came home to visit his mother. (Johnny used to work on a tramp steamer which took him to places that only existed in my imagination.)

My glance followed Kenny and Gimpie, the dog barking excitedly as Kenny climbed out of his reach. Gimpie stood up on his hindlegs pawing at the rock until Kenny threw a stick and he went racing after it. I watched them. There was a calm strength and sensibleness about this youngest son that the other children lacked. In another four or five years he'd probably be like his older brother, Marcus, who at fifteen had become quite an accomplished rugby player.

At ten Kenny was still small, much like I had been at his age, although he had his mother's grey eyes and dark brown hair. The thought of Celia knotted my stomach. She is still the most beautiful woman I have ever known. When I was young my mother used to warn me that there had to be more to a person than mere good looks. But she never had any occasion to complain about Celia who was not only beautiful, but also a good mother and a gentle, loving and supportive wife.

Of course Mama was right about looks not being everything. I always tried to encourage my children to look beyond the surface. It was difficult, though, to check outside influences in a society that still placed value on the texture of one's hair and the colour of one's skin.

Mama was disappointed that Celia and the girls had not come along on this visit. But Celia and I had talked things over, and had decided that it would be best for Kenny and me to come on our own. He was closer to Mama than any of the other children. Many of his holidays had been spent running around here at *Driehoek* with the dog in tow, while Mama doted on him.

I still worried about my mother being on her own. After the doctors had diagnosed her illness a few years ago, we feared that she might not survive another winter, but that first winter passed and so did the summer. It was now three years later and she was still with us. The only visible change was that she had aged beyond her seventy-three years. Over the last few years I had been nagged by the thought that she might not be around much longer. Hounded by these anxieties, I felt an increasing need to recapture some of the times we had shared.

I had often talked about spending a holiday here at *Driehoek* with Mama. I don't mean one of the usual hurried trips, but some meaningful time. Unfortunately, something always interfered with my plans. As a teacher, most of the short holidays were spent preparing for the following school term, so I always ended up postponing my visits. But now that my father was being released from prison I was anxious to be at home. Despite all Mama said, I still feared that with no one to restrain him she would once again fall prey to his violent temper.

It was a big help to have Kenny along. While I tinkered around, fixing things in the house, he cleaned the yard and took care of the chickens, all the light chores that Mama couldn't always manage now. In the evenings while he and Mama sat out on the *stoep*, I either chopped firewood or sat on the step smoking my pipe, quite content to listen to her telling Kenny about the old days. But my thoughts often returned to my father and the days I had spent growing up here at *Driehoek*.

I could hear the steady drone of Mama's voice almost like a counterpoint to my thoughts. She was recovering nicely but it was not without a battle from us. There were times when she was quite stubborn and irrational. For instance, she had stopped taking the medication prescribed by the doctors because, according to her, it wasn't doing her any good. Instead she was taking a herbal-tea remedy prepared by *Tante* Sinnah who lived on the far side of the valley. The

4

foul-smelling concoction permeated everything in the house, but Mama insisted that it was helping.

The first time she was taken ill, we brought her to Cape Town where the doctors put her in hospital for two weeks. After that she stayed with us for a spell while she attended an out-patient clinic. We pleaded with her to stay on afterwards but she wouldn't hear of it. In retrospect I think her anxiety to get back to *Driehoek* had something to do with my father coming home. Perhaps by that time, already, she had been expecting him to be released from prison.

'Daddy!' my son called. He ran over while Gimpie leaped up against him, trying to get hold of the stick he held high above his head. 'Is *Oupa* really coming home?' he asked.

I thought about this for a moment while my son waited for an answer. 'Yes.'

'When is he coming?'

'This week.'

'But what day?'

'I don't know, son.' I could feel a warm flush of irritation rising along my neck. Luckily Kenny turned away to throw the stick.

'Mummy says we can't love without forgiveness and compassion,' he said.

I got to my feet, placed my pipe in my mouth and stared distractedly over my son's head into the distance. I didn't share any of my wife's charitable feelings towards my father.

Mama wasn't much for going to church, but my wife Celia was a staunch Catholic and it was from her that Kenny got his spiritual training. I worried about her zeal for religion, especially when she expressed the hope that Kenny would some day enter a seminary. This was our only point of contention. I wanted him to have the same choices the other children had; I didn't want him to have regrets later on; and I hoped that time would cool his, and especially his mother's, religious fervour.

'*Ouma* says you don't get along so well with *Oupa* because of what happened when you were a boy.'

5

Mama talked to Kenny about a lot of things. There were no secrets between them. They were close. 'I don't know how I feel about him,' I said. 'I'll have to wait until we're face to face.'

'Do you really think *Ouma*'s going to die?'

'*Ouma* says she feels a lot better,' I reminded him.

'What's he like?' Kenny asked.

'Who?'

'*Oupa*.'

We watched Gimpie loping back, jaws firmly clamped on the stick.

'*Oupa*'s been gone for a long time. He left here about thirty years ago and of that time eighteen years have been spent in jail. I was only fourteen when I left the farm. I didn't see much of him after that,' I explained. I suspected that my mother was once again dwelling on the 'good old days'. I couldn't remember there being any. My recollections were mainly of bad times; the misery, our poverty and my father's violence and cruelty. It was hard to believe that after all he had done to her, and to us, she could still care so much for him.

'What did he do to you when you were a boy?' Kenny enquired, curiously.

'Let's get back. *Ouma* might be worried about us,' I said avoiding his questioning eyes.

After a moment of silence he asked: 'If *Ouma* dies, does it mean that I won't be able to visit *Driehoek* any more?'

I shrugged perfunctorily.

The dog agitated for more games and Kenny threw the stick again.

'What about Ousis, could I visit her during the holidays if *Ouma* dies?'

'Why the hell are you worrying about all of this?' I demanded, then immediately regretted my impatience. 'Your *Ouma* is healthier now than she's been for a long time.'

Hurt by the sharpness in my tone, Kenny skipped ahead, chased by the dog. The two of them eventually disappeared from view over the crest of the hill.

When we got home Mama was waiting for us on the *stoep*. 'Horace,' she said, tying her *doek* around her head, 'one of these days I want you to drive me in your car to the top of the hill so I can see the valley.'

'Whenever you're ready,' I said.

Kenny and I sat on the *stoep*. She was quiet and pensive, her thoughts obviously miles away. 'Did you have a good rest?' I asked.

She shook her head. 'I'll have all the rest I need when the time comes,' she said, squinting into the bright light.

We sat in silence watching a festival of insects which buzzed around the flower-beds. In the front yard the chickens pecked incessantly, stopping intermittently to stare with one eye whenever there was a movement from the *stoep*. Occasionally the peace was disrupted by a wild commotion in the backyard; feathers flying as Gimpie went after the old hens.

Whenever the weather allowed, we sat out enjoying the lukewarm rays of the autumn sun. There wasn't much to do around the house any more. Before I came Mama had hired some of the men to add a new roof, the house had been painted, the *stoep* repaired, and a new window put in. She was quite comfortable and more reluctant than ever to forfeit her independence, especially after Pik van der Merwe had given her life rights to the house. I would have liked to think that he did this in recognition of the thankless task Mama had looking after him and his brothers when they were children, but knowing that he was incapable of such altruism I put it down to pressure from his mother who had a soft spot for Mama.

'It's time for my medicine. Put the kettle on,' she said to Kenny.

Kenny groaned anticipating the awful smell.

'How are you feeling, Mama?' I asked.

She nodded her head and sighed.

Kenny returned and came to sit by me. We watched her in silence.

'I'm so glad the two of you could come. I may not be around for much longer,' she said.

7

Kenny turned his anguished glance to me. He didn't like her to talk like this.

I placed my hand on his shoulder and squeezed lightly. He kept his eyes averted from his grandmother, leaning his head back against my shoulder, toying with a dead leaf. Finally he crushed the leaf and blew the bits of debris into the air.

'You've been a good boy, Kenny. You take after your Daddy, did you know that?'

Kenny was silent.

'Your Daddy didn't turn out too bad, so make sure you listen to him,' she continued.

Kenny mumbled something under his breath, lowered his head and scratched Gimpie's ear.

'Come over here to *Ouma*,' she said to Kenny.

He went over and leaned against her rocking-chair.

I watched them, remembering my own childhood, and the way Mama's youthful smile used to light up her face like a ray of sunlight brightening a darkened landscape; the richness of her brown skin, and the rounded fullness of her cheeks glowing with a creamy sheen; her breath fresh with the scent of orange peel which she used to chew like some folks chewed tobacco.

Memories of my boyhood flooded back. I was no older than Kenny. Mama was sitting on the *stoep* like a lady, her hands lightly resting in her lap. Beautiful hands with long, slender fingers which were work-hardened, calloused and scaly from neglect. She'd sit there quietly rocking while I sat on the step watching her.

'If anything should ever happen to me, Horace,' she'd say, 'you make sure your brother and sister are taken care of.'

When there was no response from me she'd scowl and stop her rocking. My silence was filled with dread at the thought of something happening to her.

'Do you hear me, Horace?' Mama would ask again.

'Yes, Mama,' I'd whisper when I got back my voice.

'Cat got your tongue, son? I can't hear you.'

'Yes, Mama,' I'd say again, loud and clear.

8

Mama's voice broke into my thoughts. I glanced up to find her short-sightedly peering at me.

'Remember when you were six years old and you went out into the fields for the first time?' she asked me. Then squeezing Kenny's hand, she said, 'Your daddy started in the fields when he was just knee-high.'

At that time it was an accepted way of life for the children to work out in the fields, just as it was for the men to beat their wives, or to go out on a drinking spree which lasted from Friday afternoon to Sunday morning.

I was six the first time I waited alongside Daddy at the collection point in the vineyards. But even at that tender age I already sensed the tensions out there. I remember on my first day, Daddy was like a tightly coiled spring. First there was the inevitable argument with Aapie, the head picker, then he almost got into a fist fight with one of the other men. I thought for sure things would get out of hand and that somebody would be hurt. I couldn't help hoping that he would be the one.

'Don't worry,' Mama had said reassuringly, misinterpreting my anxiety. 'They're just blowing off steam.'

When the lorry arrived I saw that a white man was driving. No doubt this was Koos Kleinhans. I knew him instinctively from the way the men spoke about him in low tones when they got their pay and found that they had been short-changed by him. Generally the drivers were fair, the exception being this man who took perverse pleasure in regularly cheating the workers out of a portion of their earnings.

The lorry pulled up to where the boxes were stacked, ready for the pick-up. When the workers saw who was driving that day, there was the usual grumbling, sighing and rolling of eyes. The tension had already gathered like a storm cloud.

Kleinhans shouted abuse at those who stood around waiting for him. 'You *donders*, don't you have any work to do?'

At this Daddy's eyes glazed over and his expression tightened. The others waited scuffing their old boots in the

9

sand, while Kleinhans' cheeks and chest puffed up like an adder's. Instead of backing the lorry right up to the boxes, he had parked some distance away so that the workers were obliged to haul the heavy boxes to the lorry.

A few brave souls laughed or joked with him, but they did so with deference, always calling him '*Baas*' and always keeping their eyes averted, their expressions a combination of self-abasement and sly, toothless grins. At times a pathetic desperation lurked behind those servile masks.

Although Daddy never looked Koos Kleinhans in the eye, he never quite degraded himself in the same way. That much I must concede. He was silent, always with that brooding expression. He never smiled, even when Kleinhans taunted him. He was as inflexible here as he was at home, and after a particularly rough day with Kleinhans I knew that we would all have a hellish evening.

I will never forget one incident. I had been there for a few weeks only and one afternoon I was standing beside Willem at the collection point waiting for the others to finish loading the lorry. I couldn't help staring at Kleinhans and when he became aware of my scrutiny, he asked: 'Who are you *hotnot*?'

'He's Simon Jacobs' boy, *Baas*,' Willem replied quickly.

'I'm talking to him, not you, you *verdomde bobbejaan*!' Kleinhans growled.

I was petrified.

'Answer me are you Simon's boy, *hotnot*?'

My voice deserted me and I was certain he could hear my knees knocking. He waited for my response and I opened my mouth as if to answer but no sound came. Terror-stricken I raised my head and looked up at him, nodding slowly like a marionette. I was too young, and my experience with Whites too limited, to know that we did not look a white man in the eye (this lesson I was to learn much later). Eventually I wrested my glance from his. It slipped to his heavy jowls, down his stubby arms to the turn-ups of his khaki shorts. From there it slid along the two hefty, white stumps, matted with dark hair, became trapped in the thick woollen socks and finally came to rest on the tip of the *veldskoen* pressed on the running-board of the lorry.

'I'm talking to you,' he growled again.

Willem had come up beside me and with a solid clout to the side of my head said, 'Say "*Ja Baas*" to *Baas* Kleinhans.'

I glanced at the man's face and I saw that look in his eyes. It was one that I was to encounter many times in the course of my life. I hesitated, but when I saw through the corner of my eye that Willem was preparing for another swat my response was quick. '*Ja Baas!*' I cried.

The white man laughed, slapping his hairy thighs while I continued my wide-eyed scrutiny.

In a way I was glad that it was only Willem who had cuffed me; I would have been mortified had it been Daddy. He, however, was standing apart from us, his eyes averted, dissociating himself from this exchange.

'*Maak gou, jou verdomde hotnot*,' Kleinhans growled at Daddy who was moving with slow deliberate movements. The more Kleinhans shouted for him to hurry, the slower Daddy became until his movements were awkward and stilted like those of a robot. Kleinhans always called us *hotnot*. It was one of the derogatory terms created by one group to humiliate another. Their actions were not enough, they also found it necessary to attack us with words. It didn't matter whether your name was *Simon van der Stel*,* if your face was brown, you were still 'his *hotnot*,' or 'a *hotnot*' or just plain '*hotnot*'.

Daddy kept his head down and lifted the boxes of grapes onto the back of the lorry, his face frozen in that same inscrutable expression.

*Dutch East Indian company commander arrived in South Africa in 1679.

11

TWO

The rhythmic thumping of the rocker had ceased and I suddenly became aware of the silence. Startled, I glanced up. Mama and Kenny were grinning, obviously amused by my preoccupation.

'Your Daddy's in dreamland again,' Mama said to Kenny.

'Sorry, I was just thinking about the old days,' I responded sheepishly. 'What were you saying?'

'I asked you about Sissie. Is she coming home?' she asked.

I shook my head. 'I haven't been able to get hold of her.'

'I want you to telephone the mission in Swaziland again,' she said. 'What's wrong with that girl? First she says she's coming for a holiday, then we don't hear another word from her again.'

'I'll drive into town this afternoon and book a person-to-person phone call from the post office again.'

'You can ask Pik van der Merwe. He'll let you use the phone. He's not a bad person. He's got more heart than his daddy ever had. You drive over there and tell him that your Mama sent you to use the telephone.'

'I'd rather go into town,' I argued.

'You go to the farmhouse and you tell *Baas* Pik that I sent you,' she said sternly. There was no use arguing. To her I was still a little boy.

I had no intention of dealing with Pik van der Merwe, and my days of '*Ja Baasing*' were over. Besides, there would always be a lingering resentment towards that family. I could not forget that for all those years Mama had spent her time taking care of the white children while we were left to our own devices.

Sometimes when I think about it, a tight feeling fills my chest. I had tried to convince myself so often that we had no choice in those days; that it was in the past anyway, that now things had changed and that we were no longer subservient to the van der Merwe dynasty. But it didn't help. The bitterness lingered, even though as youngsters Pik and I had run off to the dam at every opportunity to strip and cavort together, oblivious to our differences in skin colour. Awareness came a few years later when they were sent off to boarding school. Our escapades often ended in punishment, but we'd be back again. I remember how Pik, who was younger than I, used to tag along after us, stubbornly resisting the stones and threats designed to chase him back. There was always trouble when he came along. Mama used to say it was because he was younger and his mother feared for his safety with all our reckless pranks.

Mama sighed. She was obviously still thinking about Sissie. I had tried every possible means to get hold of my sister. I'd made several phone calls to Swaziland already but no one at the mission in Mbabane knew where she was. Apparently she had gone north to some of the villages and there was no way of reaching her.

'I know you've tried, Horace. I know,' Mama sighed, toying with the edge of her handkerchief. 'I've always been able to depend on you.'

I glanced away, racked by guilt that my help had come so late. When she needed me most in those early years, I had neglected her in pursuit of my own interests.

I had intended to send for her after I got married, even though she had made it clear that she would never leave her home here at *Driehoek* to live in Cape Town. Lately I'd been wondering whether I'd tried hard enough to convince her otherwise. After our first child, Marcus, the two girls had come in quick succession and we had all been crowded into a small two-bedroom flat. Six years later we were still living under those crowded conditions and I was still nurturing the hope of having Mama to live with us one day.

I know she had tried to do her best for us, acting as a buffer between my father and us. I was barely nine when Daddy started agitating that it was time for me to pull my weight. Mama argued that I was too young, but since her opinion carried no weight around our house, his will prevailed.

13

Luckily I was small for my age (most children in the valley were undernourished), and the overseer refused to put me on the payroll. I was more fortunate than most of the children; I had another two-year reprieve from the long hours of back-breaking work in the fields.

On my eleventh birthday Mama ran out of excuses and Daddy insisted that it was time. She pleaded with him to let me at least finish Standard Four. This dream to educate me and Sissie was all she had left.

The only opportunity we had for escape was when Boetie Kiewiet and I ran off to the dam to seek respite from the unending drudgery in the vineyards. The dam still stands. A gritty mud wall on one side, a grass-covered slope on the other with willow branches drooping down to break the surface of the water. On hot summer days we used to grab handfuls of the springy branches and swing out like monkeys, letting go to splash into the muddy water.

Sometimes when we forgot about returning to finish the chores, Daddy would be waiting for me with the *sjambok*, or with a whip picked from the quince tree. But all the punishment in the world was no deterrent for those few hours of boyhood pleasure.

When I turned twelve and finished my Standard Four at the farm school, I informed Mama that I was perfectly capable of doing a man's job and that it was no longer necessary for her to protect me from Daddy. I explained that it was more important for Sissie, who was two years younger than me and much smarter, to continue her schooling. I also saw no point in getting myself educated just so that I could labour in the fields. Mama realised that with me working, it would only be a matter of time before it occurred to Daddy that Sissie could also be gainfully employed in the fields.

'I'll kill him if he takes her out of school,' she vowed.

I knew that she was no more capable of killing him than she was of wringing the necks of the chickens, a task which had fallen to Sissie and me. My sister and I became secretive. Learning to obtain by stealth what would be denied in open confrontation.

14

When I left school I kept some of my books, hiding them under my bed so that Daddy never found out about Mama and Sissie who had tried to keep up my education at home. He had had no education. He couldn't read or write his name and he resented the fact that his children were better educated than he. One day, however, the rats got to the books and all that was left was a pile of confetti.

There was no hope of replacing those books. Our combined earnings at *Driehoek*, after paying off something on our debts, were barely enough to keep us from starving. The enormous burden of our liabilities to Andries van der Merwe enslaved us. Many of our debts were incurred in the trading store owned by him.

Everyone I had spoken to recently, agreed that things had changed since Pik van der Merwe had taken over the running of the farm from his father. In Andries van der Merwe's days there were about twenty families legally employed at *Driehoek*. They lived in stone houses built more than a hundred years ago. The rest of the community was made up of squatters and itinerant workers who camped in crude shelters during harvest time, working all over the valley wherever there was a job available. Some of them had squatted here at *Driehoek* for at least two generations.

These people had become part of the community despite occasional conflicts which flared up between those who were legally employed and had a proportion of their salary deducted for rent, and the others who were not subject to such deductions. The squatters on the other hand were vulnerable to police raids and were often forcibly moved, their shacks torn down in the process. But as soon as the police were gone the squatters returned to rebuild their shacks again.

When money ran out, food and essentials were bought on credit. One thing about Andries van der Merwe, he never stinted with his credit. The deeper the workers were indebted to him, the greater his hold over them.

At the end of the harvest the men worked at other jobs, either in the wine cellars as coopers, repairing and making the casks and barrels used in the winery, or labouring in the barns, or on the land: cutting, pruning, spraying young plants, ploughing and working the irrigation ditches. Off-season the women generally kept the big white house with its twelve bedrooms clean and running efficiently. In addition Mama's responsibility included taking care of the van der Merwe children. Then, sometimes after finishing her own work Mama went out to help Daddy with his jobs.

Nothing stopped her, not even her pregnancies. I remember one day she was out in the fields, heavy with child, still picking the grapes and carrying heavy boxes. From where I worked I kept an eye on her and whenever I saw her struggling, I rushed over to give her a hand.

'You want to lose your job, sonny? I'll lose mine for sure if that man catches you running backwards and forwards like this,' Daddy said, grabbing my arm and gesturing with his head towards the overseer.

'Ousis say she's not supposed to be carrying heavy boxes,' I said pulling my arm free.

'How would that damn woman know? She don't even have a child. Now you better stop this running around before someone sees you. Your mama is no little china doll. She's strong and healthy and some exercise won't do her no harm.'

That morning Mama gave birth to Abel while lying in an irrigation ditch out of sight of the overseer, Piet Coetzee. Fanny and Ousis Cook helped her with the delivery. After the birth Ousis wrapped the baby in her shawl and put him in the bottom of a basket while Mama went right back to work.

When it was all over I walked away to the grove of trees. That's where Marietjie found me. 'No need to be shamed,' she said, 'it's only nature. Nothing you can do about that. One day your wife will do it too, if you ever make up your mind about getting married.' She grinned and gave me a sideways, leering glance.

It was generally believed that Marietjie had a few marbles missing, so not many of us paid attention to what she said or did. Mama used to tease me saying that Marietjie liked me. I usually denied this vehemently. In reality, though, I didn't mind her. In fact sometimes I felt sorry for her, but when she was brazen and flirtatious I gave her a wide berth. I didn't want Sophie to see Marietjie carrying on like this since it was Sophie that I really liked.

During my 'Sophie Phase' I usually planned my trips to the water-tap so that they coincided with hers. I waited there until she'd filled her bucket, then watched with pulsing heart while she lifted the bucket onto her head. Sometimes she wore a dress that was torn, or too big for her, and when she raised her arms I'd catch a glimpse of those firm, tantalizing buds. At times like that a hot and uncontrollable urge swelled up inside me and I'd have to slink away behind the shed. Here, engorged and throbbing, I soon found a variety of ways to effect a quick release from my exquisite discomfort.

Sophie was beautiful. Not like Marietjie who was tall, thin and ugly. Sophie was like a plump fruit bursting with ripeness. They were both about my age, but the two girls were so different that I didn't dare mention them in the same breath. Whenever I complained about Marietjie hanging around me all the time, Mama told me that looks weren't everything. But sometimes by the way she said this, I thought that not even she was quite convinced in Marietjie's case.

'She has something special,' Miss Stoffels assured us one day when Mama and I were discussing Marietjie's lack of attributes.

'Like what?' I asked sceptically. There were times when Miss Stoffels stood up so fiercely for Marietjie that one was too afraid to criticise her.

'She was born with a helm,' Miss Stoffels told me.

I looked at Mama for an explanation.

'I helped to bring her into the world, and I remember the helm quite distinctly,' Miss Stoffels continued.

'Mama, what's a helm?' I asked.

'It's a caul; a second skin over the baby's head. People think that a baby born like that has special powers,' Mama explained.

Miss Stoffels, fearing that the discussion might lead to other questions relating to birth, quickly changed the subject. In those days topics about birth were relegated to the domain of married women and never mentioned in the presence of children, especially not male children. Yet in far-flung communities like ours, birth and death were often inter-twined; the young expected to help when no one else was available.

Miss Stoffels continued to look at Mama with that self-righteous expression. Mama seemed not to notice. She was better educated than most of the women in the valley and in some ways a bit superior, although she tried never to show it. But in my mind there was no doubt that she was superior to every one of them. Formerly Miss Naomi Abrams from Paarl, Mama completed her Junior Certificate there and would have entered Normal College, had she not met my father who was a builder at that time.

After she and Daddy were married, they ended up here. His father, *Oupa* Jacobs, had worked at *Driehoek* as a cooper for most of his life, as had his father before him. *Oupa* Jacobs was the one who encouraged my father to come out when there was a shortage of construction work. But he died soon after my mother and father arrived; then Daddy was obliged to work to pay off *Oupa*'s debts to van der Merwe. In the process of doing this my father himself became indebted. At times when Mama and Daddy quarrelled, she'd say some harsh things to him about the way her life had turned out and he'd silence her with a single blow to her mouth.

My mother was a gentle person. This gentleness was more evident than ever in the way she treated Abel, the youngest, who was born out in the field. He had something wrong with him, you could tell by just looking at him. Mama once took him to a doctor in Cape Town who said that part of his brain had been damaged during birth. Miss Stoffels thought the damage had been caused by the poisonous sprays, but it was really the beatings. Daddy kept on beating her even when she was heavy with child. Mama had come to the farm determined to retain some vestige of dignity and pride but he broke her like a horse. We all learnt what it was like to be exposed to a father who used brutality to instil fear when respect could not be gained.

For fear that Abel would be torn from her like the rest of us, she took him everywhere with her. In the mornings she'd leave home with him strapped to her back, even during harvest season when everyone was busy. Out in the fields while the women picked, we children helped the men to chase the birds, making loud noises and flicking our whips high above the vines. We were so busy that there was hardly time to feed Abel. He cried constantly then.

When he was bigger, Mama let him play in the ground at her feet. Sometimes she put a bunch of grapes in her pocket along with the other fruit and vegetable peelings collected from the van der Merwe's kitchen. There were always piles of curly citrus strips amidst the bounty of fruit and vegetable peelings which dried on the roof of the shack beside our house. The birds carried some of it away but there was still enough of the dried peelings for us. Mama counted us lucky that she had access to the van der Merwe's discards.

Mama always used to save something for me to eat when I visited her at the van der Merwe's house. But I was banished from the big house after Mrs van der Merwe saw me taking the pocket-knife from the kitchen dresser. Mama had to do some pretty fancy talking to get me out of that spot. Luckily for me she didn't tell Daddy. It would have been one more excuse for him to beat me. When I saw that knife I knew it was exactly what I needed to cut him up the next time he laid a hand on us.

Mama clouted me when we got outside and my ears burnt with righteous indignation. 'What do you think you were doing?' she demanded. 'You want old Andries van der Merwe to kick us off the farm. Where will we go? For Lord's sake Horace, use your sense.' Then she clouted me again.

I was so filled with resentment, that at that moment I felt she deserved everything she got from my father. Fortunately it was a temporary state which soon passed.

THREE

It seemed that we'd come full cycle. Here we were thirty years later and Mama was again waiting for that old son-of-a-bitch. I couldn't understand her reasoning and my blood boiled when I thought of him, and of Mama waiting for him.

One morning on my way to town Aapie flagged me down. He used to be the head picker during Daddy's days. He was about eighty now; a tall, lean and sinewy man. Despite the trembling walk which slowed him down, his spotless, carefully groomed appearance carried a reminder of an earlier grace. The debilitating effect of St Vitus's dance, however, was taking its toll. Everything shook and rattled including the set of false teeth which had formerly belonged to Oumisies van der Merwe. These were so large that they slipped, slid and clattered like old bones each time he moved his head. They were useless for any practical purpose other than vanity.

Aapie told me that it was a good thing I had passed by when I did because he was just on his way to see me. Thinking he wanted a lift, I told him to get in. But he shook his head and leaned through the open window, resting his elbows on the door.

'I thought you should know,' he said, his clacking teeth sounding like a pair of castanets. He turned his head and spat a stream of red juice into the sand. 'I seen your daddy.'

'Where?' I asked, startled.

'There by Carelse's old shack.' He straightened up and pointed beyond the hills to where Kerel Carelse's old corrugated-iron shanty still graced the earth.

'Are you sure, *Boet* Aapie?' I asked.

'*Ja*, man. I saw him with my own two eyes. I was getting a ride on Lucas's donkey-cart to Kiewiet's farm when I saw smoke coming from a cook fire. Well, you know *mos*, no one's been staying there in the shack since Kerel died. So I told Lucas to stop the cart. I went over there. I can see very good with these eyes still. Never wore glasses or anything in my life only my teeth … '

'You saw my daddy?' I interrupted, guiding him back on to the track again.

'*Ooh. Nou ja.* I would know him anywhere.'

'Did you speak to him?'

'No. He took off like a rabbit when he sees me. So I says to Lucas: "Never mind, when he feels like having company, he can come to the quarters. He knows his way, *ne*? A man don't forget his way home." I tell you first, before your mama hears about it.'

I nodded and thanked him. 'I want you to do me a favour.'

'*Ja?*' he asked, leaning forward and sucking his teeth back into place.

'Don't tell anyone that you saw him. Not for a few days anyway.'

Puzzled, he looked at me.

I said I needed some time to prepare Mama or it might come as too much of a shock to her. The truth of course, was that I wanted to see him first, wanted to warn him away. We didn't need him hanging around and Mama didn't need the heartache.

Aapie wasn't too happy about my request but agreed to keep the secret for a few more days, or at least for one more day. 'Someone else is bound to see him,' he warned.

'That's all right, *Boet* Aapie. Don't worry about it,' I said.

Instead of going into town, I drove directly over to the shack. The place looked deserted, but after poking around outside I could tell that it had been used by a succession of down-and-outs.

There was a lot of rubbish strewn about, some old tyres and a rusted metal bed-frame were leaning against the sheet of zinc which formed one of the walls. Inside an old blanket lay crumpled on the floor; beside it was a mug and a chipped enamel pot. There was no window, only a doorway. With the wind blowing in through this opening and coming in through the gaps between the sheets of corrugated zinc, I knew that it would be cold at night. Winter was just around the corner.

I returned to the car where I sat waiting for him, rehearsing the things I would say, the anger and bitterness building up,

21

straining and pushing like a dam about to burst. I remembered the beatings and hated him more than ever. It was best for me to leave now, I decided, or I might not be responsible for my actions. I started the car and backed up to turn around. I was just about to drive away when I saw an old man, grey and stooped, struggling towards me. He was limping, leaning on his *kierie*.

Shocked, I realised that this old wreck of a man was my father. Our glances met and he raised a hand in greeting. It remained there, poised in mid-air. I saw all this in the rear-view mirror as I sped by. He half turned, dropped his hand and stood staring after the car. In a moment he was swallowed up in my dust.

When I got home Mama was sitting on the *stoep* staring out as though expecting someone other than me.

'Who are you waiting for?' I asked irritably.

'No one,' she said shortly.

I was still shaken by the encounter with my father. I sat on the step, thoughtfully taking my pipe from my pocket. I didn't want to tell her just yet. I wanted to go back there one more time. I had prepared everything so well, all the things I was going to tell him and now none of it seemed appropriate. The image I had carried around in my head was a childhood memory which differed greatly from the reality of the incapacitated old man I had just seen.

'Did you get hold of Sissie?' Mama asked.

I shook my head. I couldn't utter the lie. I hadn't gone into town.

Mama was still concerned about Sissie. She had worried from the moment I received that letter in which Sissie wrote that she was thinking of visiting me. She and I still corresponded on a regular basis. I kept her abreast of Mama's condition. I knew that she would come eventually, but Mama was impatient.

'She'll come when she can,' I said.

'You ring her and tell her to come soon, or else ... '

'I thought you said you were feeling much better,' I

protested. 'Besides I told you she's not in Mbabane. They don't know where she is.'

Mama disdainfully returned her attention to the distant horizon.

Later that afternoon Marietjie provided some distraction when she stopped by for a visit. I hadn't had a chance to call on her yet. The only friends seen since my arrival home were the ones met at the Good Friday service held in the school-house.

Marietjie and I talked for a while. Mama was very quiet and I was a little worried about her. 'So much is still going to happen in this place,' Marietjie whispered wearily. She touched Mama's brow and sighed. 'This valley is cursed.'

'*Ag*, nonsense with you Marietjie. You people and your damned curses. Stop worrying about Jerry. He'll be all right. He's a big boy,' Mama said impatiently. Then turning towards me, she explained: 'Marietjie thinks that something bad's going to happen to the boy. He's quite safe where he is in Lambert's Bay. He's got a job and everything so I don't know why she's worrying about him.'

Marietjie shook her head dejectedly. I watched Marietjie and Mama together. Marietjie had the same sad defeated look in her eyes that I had seen in the eyes of the other women.

Sissie always rejected the notion that it was noble to suffer. She had probably known this long before it ever occurred to me. She was so full of contradictions, it was enough to make your head spin. The day she left to become a missionary in Swaziland, she vowed never to return to this country. 'I'm tired of the struggle,' she had told me once. 'I want to be where God's word can take root on fertile ground.'

Mama used to scoff about this, saying that it was just a lot of Bible-thumping shit which taught us to turn the other cheek. 'The Bible is the white man's tool,' she used to say. 'When the white man came to these shores, he had the Bibles and the Blacks had the land. Now he has the land and they have the Bibles.'

Sissie would get mad but only because this truth came from Mama. Ousis said that towards the end before Sissie ran off to

23

become a missionary, she and Mama used to fight worse than Mama and Daddy. 'All because your Mama took your Daddy back again,' she said.

I couldn't get the image of the old man out of my mind. To think that on so many occasions I had feared for her life at his hands. It seemed that there was always someone pushing down on her. If it wasn't Daddy it was someone else like Piet Coetzee. He was the one who told Mama never to bring Abel to the vineyards again. It happened the day Abel crawled off to sit in the shade under the lorry. Had one of the labourers not seen him he would surely have been run over and killed that day.

Piet Coetzee blamed Mama for the near mishap.

'What am I to do? I can't leave him at home alone,' she cried outraged.

Mama couldn't bear the thought of Sissie staying at home with Abel, but she couldn't stop work; she needed the income to feed us. The little bit she managed to hide from Daddy she hoped would someday buy us our ticket to freedom.

At first she left Abel at home in one of the wooden boxes in which the grapes were carried. Between us we managed to rig up a contraption to which a bottle of sugar water could be attached at the side of the box. By merely turning his head, Abel could reach the big tit which he sucked on all day long until Sissie got home. Later on when Abel got a little older, I built a pen out of chicken-wire on the *stoep*. During the day Abel was left by himself with his bottle and a few crusts of bread.

After school Sissie took care of him, loving him and cleaning him up so that Mama never saw the flies sticking to the glue which dribbled from his nose or crawled into his mouth when he was asleep; neither did she see the crusted mess in his napkin. By the time Mama got home, Sissie even had the fire made and a black enamel pot of mealie-meal pap cooking on the stove.

Sissie was like a little mother to Abel. When he was hurt, it was she he ran to, not Mama. All day long he stumbled around in his small cage on the *stoep*, and when he had exhausted himself crying he fell asleep.

Daddy couldn't stand being around Abel. At times he also sought refuge behind the shed, but for different reasons of course. I remember the shock I had one day when panting with ardour after an encounter with Sophie, I rushed off to my spot only to find Daddy sitting on the log, smoking. Shocked, I stood stock still for several agonising moments, hoping that he wouldn't notice the way the front of my short trousers bulged out.

'*Wat soek jy?*' he growled, demanding to know what I wanted.

I was too startled to move.

'Come here.'

Slowly one scaly foot came up rubbing the calf of the other leg. I kept my eyes on him, chewing on my bottom lip, the rents in my trousers flapping in the breeze, my passion mercifully cooling.

Sissie hated Daddy with a frightening intensity. She predicted that he would go straight to Hell when he died, and the way she described Hell, it was no place that I ever wanted to go – with snakes, fire and dark pits. There were no half measures with her. She was always full of fire. Her brown eyes were like the colour of golden-syrup; blazing with anger one moment, and the next sparkling with laughter. It was ironical that of all people, Sissie had inherited Daddy's physical features. She was dark like him with his kinky hair. In character, though, she was more like Mama with the same gentle and caring qualities.

No matter how much Mama loved Abel, it was Sissie who brought that spark of life to Abel's eyes, and when he was too old to be on her lap, she sat him on the step beside her, his hand in hers.

Then one day Abel took ill. His eyes filled with a feverish brightness and he grew thinner each day. His face became gaunt and expressionless and a steady stream of spittle dribbled down his chin. He couldn't do a thing for himself;

25

neither speak nor wipe his face. Every time Daddy saw him he'd fly into a rage, and at these times he could quite easily have kicked Abel right off the step where he sat with old Dog licking the spittle off his chin.

Sometimes when Mama stood by the door to watch Sissie with Abel, a look of such infinite sadness would pass over her face that I wanted to reach out to comfort her; to tell her what a good mother she's been to all of us. In the end Abel died of pneumonia. Some people said it was just as well but Sissie was inconsolable. I think at that time something inside her crystallised because she was never the same again.

Some Saturdays when Daddy went over to Meisie's to hang around the *shebeen*, a breath of fresh air blew through the house. With him gone we'd all laugh and joke and have a good time, carrying on as if we didn't have a care in the world.

On the last Saturday of every month the burial society representative, who travelled around the coloured communities in the Boland, came around and Mama would always say the same thing to him: 'Why should I pay good money to travel in style to the next life when my children are starving in this one?'.

The man was a red-faced, fat Afrikaner who waited out in his car while his clients came to him, money tightly clutched in their sweaty palms. Although reluctant to part with their money, they wanted the benefits of belonging to a burial society. After the people had all gone we'd watch him counting the coins, stacking them into neat little piles, scrutinising those that were worn and hammered out of shape.

'No-good damn *Boer*,' Mama used to mutter under her breath. 'That's what happens to parasites. They get big and fat like ticks.' We knew about ticks. Sometimes we had the unpleasant task of picking them off Dog when he came from the *veld*.

My mother stood in the open door for hours watching as the others parted with their last few shillings hoping that it would secure a decent journey into the other world. But there were always some who despite their contributions, ended up in

26

makeshift coffins anyway. Most people were too far from a bank or a society office for the family to make appropriate arrangements; in other cases illiterate relatives were unable to file a claim. Others were too timid to assert their rights, just as they were too timid to stand up to Andries van der Merwe or Koos Kleinhans.

'If I ever die,' Mama would say loud enough for the representative to hear, 'you make sure you bury me in a plain plank box. It's all the same to me. You hear Horace?' When the red-faced Afrikaner scowled, she'd grin and shut the door.

We'd have a good laugh about this behind the closed door. 'Did you see his face with his fat little froggy cheeks?' Mama would cry, puffing her cheeks, her eyes bulging with mirth. Sissie and I would interject too, holding our sides as we recalled something that was worth recounting.

But things weren't always this jolly. Sometimes Daddy stayed at home instead of going out to the *shebeen* with the other men. At times like this the atmosphere at home was charged with tension.

I remember one night when Abel was still alive, Daddy stayed home instead of joining the others at Meisie's place. Mama had made some wine, and Daddy was sitting on the *stoep*. The light from the moon brightened things up outside and with the lamplight shining through the window I could see him quite clearly. Abel was also there, sitting to one side, his mouth hanging open, drooling as usual. He seemed to be mesmerised by the light shining through the translucent amber fluid in the bottle. My father became aware of Abel's gaze, and turned his head.

In his drunken frame of mind, it didn't take much for him to get worked up. His bloodshot eyes glared at my brother, his brows coming together to form deep furrows before a look of utter digust settled over his expression. I knew that I had to get Abel away from him, but I was afraid to move. Abel smiled and turned his head to one side like a curious monkey. I saw Daddy's eyes narrowing, and my heart pushed up into my mouth.

'The next time you sit staring at me like this,' he growled, 'I'll cut you up and feed you to the crows, you goddamn half-witted bastard.'

But he made no move towards my brother, he just sat there with the bottle in his hand, staring Abel down. Abel was smiling in that peculiar way of his, his head turned to one side. I inched over to the *stoep* and reached out for Abel's hand. Abel resisted but I pulled him away, taking him to the relative safety of the house.

FOUR

'Why didn't you tell me that your daddy was living in the old shack?' Mama asked.

I turned away from that aggrieved expression in her eyes and gazed into the distance.

'Why, Horace? Why did you have to do this to me? Why?'

'I thought ... '

'He's an old man. What harm can he do? You went to see him and you never told me.'

'I didn't speak to him. I just drove by.'

'Ousis says *Boet* Aapie saw him and he told you about it. She says he's an old man, doubled up with arthritis, hardly able to move one foot ahead of the other. Can't you find it in your heart to forgive him? He is your father!' The tears left damp tracks down her cheeks.

'I'll take you there,' I said quietly.

'No,' she said. 'I'll wait right here for him to come to me. He knows where his home is.'

Mama made no bones about being upset with me. With a sense of irony I accepted her reproach. It was hard to believe that a man of my age, with a family of my own, could still be chastised like a little boy. I resolved that one of these days I would explain that I only had her best interests at heart.

'I see your mama's still upset with you,' Ousis remarked when she called in the following afternoon. She had come to visit Mama who had fallen asleep on the sofa, so Ousis joined me out on the step. It was the first opportunity we had had to talk.

Ousis was an enormous woman, heavy hipped and big bosomed; always mopping her face and neck even in the cool winter temperatures. As a child I had always wondered what it would be like to carry around all that extra weight, her breasts protruding like twin udders.

'Naomi's upset about you not telling her your daddy was here in the valley.' She tut-tutted and shook her head. 'That

29

wasn't too clever. You know how fast the news travels in these parts.'

I shrugged.

'I hear he's just skin and bone, crippled by arthritis.'

'I don't have much sympathy for him, Ousis. I can't forget what we went through with him. Not only Mama, but all of us.'

'Your mama says he's a harmless old fool now. She says its time you put the past to rest. She wants you to forgive him.'

I glanced away.

'He won't be around for much longer.'

'Look, Ousis, I don't want to talk about him. Now if you want to talk, let's talk about something else, otherwise I have things to do.' I had no intention of sitting there listening to her plead my father's case.

'You're a good man. Not like the others. Naomi did a real good job with you, despite your daddy,' Ousis said shrewdly. 'Celia is a lucky woman to get a husband like you. By the way, how is she?'

'Fine,' I said.

'And how are the rest of the children?'

'Fine. They're all fine.'

'I saw Kenny over at Jannie's house. The two boys get along so well.'

'*Ja*,' I muttered.

'I thought Celia would come to visit your mama,' she said in an off-hand way.

'We thought it best for me and Kenny to come so that we could stay a while.'

'Uh huh.'

'Someone had to stay with the other children.'

'Naomi told me about the fine house you have in Catkin Estates,' she continued.

I chuckled. 'Catkin Estates in some ways is no better than *Driehoek*. The only difference is that there, at least, the houses have windows. Thank God, otherwise it would be like living in the middle of the Kalahari. Hot, dry and sandy. The wind carries the dust and when that sun hits you can hear it zinging off the iron roof. It's nothing fancy, Ousis. A small two-bed-roomed house, hardly big enough for all of us.'

Ousis turned to me in surprise. 'I thought with you being a teacher things would be better.'

I shook my head. 'Things are the same for all the non-Whites. You can never pull yourself up. Every time you crawl up from the sewer to see the light, the government slams the lid back over your head.'

'Don't I know,' Ousis said, giving me a long hard look.

But I knew that she really didn't understand. How could they, who had spent all their lives here in isolation, know any better? Thank God, my mother had had the presence of mind to send me away, and to think she had practically had to chase me off with a broomstick.

I remembered I had been working full time in the fields for three years already. At fourteen I was still puny, but determined to show my father that I could do a man's job. There were times when I regretted that I wasn't big and strong like Benny. Although he was only sixteen he went everywhere with the older men. He even accompanied them to the *shebeen* on Friday nights. Ousis said that it was sinful the way the men were showing Benny the road to hell.

One Friday night which was my last night at *Driehoek*, my father came home drunk as a lord, and broke Mama's arm. I tried to stop him. I climbed on his back, kicking and pummelling, struggling to drag him off her. But he was a strong man and picked me off him like a nit, flinging me against the wall. I saw more stars that night than I'd seen in my entire life.

Sissie was the only one who came through this episode unscathed. When Mama saw the trouble coming she sent her off to hide.

'If I'd had that knife tonight,' I told Mama when we sat on the *stoep* afterwards, 'he'd be dead.'

She shook her head. 'He's still your father.'

I couldn't understand how she could still be so easy on him after all he had done to her. When he stormed off I went to fetch

31

Ousis and Sissie. They put Mama's arm in a splint and patched up some of the cuts.

That incident happened a long time ago and yet the hurt was as fresh as though it had happened yesterday. I sighed wearily.

'What is it?' Ousis asked.

'I was just thinking about my father,' I said.

She studied me in silence. There was that look of wisdom in her eyes that women generally wear when they are about to make a profound statement.

I waited, but there was no response so I continued. 'Why does Mama still care for him after all this time and after everything he's done to her?'

'You don't understand, Horace. You're a man,' she said, pausing thoughtfully. 'You see, a woman doesn't take her marriage lightly. For her it's a lifetime commitment, and she sticks by him through thick and thin. It's even worse when she has children by that man. Then she's stuck to him like glue. It's like a knot that ties her to him. That man is part of each of the children. No matter how badly he treats her, she'll stick with him because he has given a part of himself to her through her children. It's the way we were made. And what you feel or say about your mother won't change the way she feels about that man.'

I shook my head in disbelief. Ousis was right. I didn't understand.

I remembered the night when he left after breaking Mama's arm and she and I sat out on the *stoep*. We were fairly safe because we knew that he wouldn't be back until Sunday afternoon.

Mama leaned against the post, her dark eyes filled with misery. 'I have a little bit of money buried out in the back yard in an old tin can. I want you to dig it up.'

'What for?' I asked.

'Take it and go to Cape Town. Ousis has a cousin there. I know she'll put you up for a while until you can finish your schooling.'

'I don't want to leave you. He'll kill you and Sissie.'

'I don't want any argument from you Horace. You do as I tell you.'

'What about him?'

'I'll take care of him.'

'I'm not going Mama.'

There was an intensity in her eyes that I had never seen before. 'You go,' she told me, grabbing me by my shirt-front with her good hand, almost choking the life out of me. 'Go dig that money up, and I'll get the address from Ousis. Jaapie's taking the wagon into Villiersdorp. I'll ask him to give you a ride. From there you can take the train to Cape Town. Find Ousis's cousin and write regularly, but don't send the letters here, send them to Ousis.'

'Mama ... '

'I don't want to hear another word.'

'He'll kill you.'

'No, he won't kill me, but after what you've done tonight I fear for your life.'

'I'm not scared of him.'

'Go and get ready; Jaapie will be leaving early in the morning. By the time that old bugger, your daddy, comes to, you'll be long gone. I'll tell him you ran off and we don't know where you are.'

I left under cover of darkness, sitting on the back of the donkey cart, hugging my small bundle of possessions. Mama and Sissie walked alongside the cart to the end of the rutted road, then stood waving until my tears and the darkness blotted them from my vision.

During the first four years Mama and Sissie wrote regularly. There was a letter from them at least once a month. They were long loving letters, but as though by design neither made any mention of how Daddy was treating them. In every letter my mother reminded me not to pick up any bad ways. I assumed that Ousis's cousin, Marie, had written to tell her that I was mixed up with a rough crowd.

Despite all the big city influences, I remained in school, and did well. Thanks to the tutoring from Mama and Sissie I advanced two years and at nineteen I had passed into Standard Nine. Mama was glad that I was planning to go to teacher's college. In one of her letters she wrote that my education had made the struggle worthwhile. Sometimes I longed for *Driehoek*, other times I was glad to be away.

In September of the following year when I turned twenty, I went home for the first time. It was more than six years since I'd seen Mama and Sissie. I had no doubt that they would be surprised to see me all grown up now. I was tall, close to six feet, but some people still thought I looked like a string-bean. I had dressed for the occasion, wanting to look my best, but also wanting in a way to reflect some of the city influence.

A pallie lent me his zoot suit and platform shoes. The *veld* hat I had borrowed from another was far too big, the brim resting uncomfortably on my ears, the only part of my anatomy that had outstripped my other development. Dressed up in my dark suit, tie and platform shoes, I felt like the prodigal son. I had informed Mama and Sissie that I was coming and was expecting them to meet me at the station.

The train arrived at noon but neither of them was there. I waited around for about an hour, enduring all sorts of curious and suspicious glances from the station workers. Finally I realised that they weren't coming. Luckily for me there was an *oompie* in a horse-drawn cart, picking up supplies for a neighbouring farm. He gave me a lift to the crossroads and from there I had to walk the ten miles to *Driehoek*.

By the time I got to the valley, my zoot suit was covered in dust, the white shirt was smeared with sweat and grime, and the heels of Mickey's shoes were shorn off on one side. My feet felt like pieces of raw flesh. I longed to take off the shoes but pride prevented me from arriving there like some barefooted *hotnot*.

The sweat poured down my face and with each step the suitcase, which held Mama and Sissie's presents, grew heavier. Eventually I removed my tie and threading this through the suitcase handle, slung it over my shoulders.

34

When I arrived at home and stood in the doorway, Sissie's face was a picture. Then she burst out laughing. I was mortified when she flicked off my hat to expose my ears; my Achilles heel, and promptly dubbed me *oortjies* – ears.

I couldn't wait to see Sophie and after spending time answering Mama and Sissie's questions I was in a hurry to strut my stuff. To my disappointment, however, I discovered that Sophie had married and left *Driehoek*. It was a relief that Daddy wasn't home. Mama said he'd found himself a young girl on one of the neighbouring farms. There was such a convivial air at home in my father's absence that I hoped he would stay away for ever.

Sissie had changed in the years that I had been away. There was a core of hardness about her that surprised me. Ousis told me about how Sissie had stood up to my father. She said that even though Daddy would never admit it, he was wary of her. According to Ousis he never beat Mama while Sissie was around. She said Sissie had warned him that if he ever touched any of them again, she'd castrate him.

I don't know whether it was her threat that had the desired effect or whether Daddy had experienced a genuine change of heart, but Mama said that the beatings had stopped.

A month after I had returned to Cape Town, I heard from Sissie that he was back home again with promises that he was a changed man. Sissie was bitterly disappointed that Mama had taken him back and said that she had had enough of Mama, Daddy and everything at *Driehoek*. She was ready to leave.

I was dismayed. I worried about Mama and what protection she'd have against my father with Sissie gone. I knew that it wouldn't be long before he was back to his old tricks again. After all a leopard never changes its spots.

Some time went by before I heard again from my sister. I couldn't get either her or Mama out of my mind. A great deal happened in the years that followed, but during the dark moments of my life, Mama's beautiful face always appeared like a beacon to lead me out of my misery.

Ousis's voice cut into my thoughts, bringing me back to the present.

'So how long are you staying for?' she asked.

'Until next Monday.'

'I wouldn't worry about Naomi too much. She's doing quite well on that medicine *Tante* Sinnah prepared for her. She'll live to a ripe old age, don't you worry. We're tough old birds, you know.'

I nodded.

'And don't worry about your daddy, neither. He's just an old man now. He can't do her no harm. Somehow we all make it one way or another. We all have our own cross to bear in life. Take Marietjie for instance,' she continued, 'she also put up with a lot. Her husband, Baba, didn't treat her no better than your daddy treated Naomi. But Marietjie stuck with him too. It's the way things are, and you can't change it, no way. Only trouble is that her boy Jerry didn't turn out so good either. Got into trouble with the gangsters in Cape Town, that's why he's in Lambert's Bay. She knows this, but she won't see any wrong in that boy. He's going to break her heart. I just know it. A few months ago they robbed a Chinaman who was running numbers for a gangster by the name of Smiley ... Do you know him?' she asked.

I shook my head.

'He's a Malay. According to Jerry, everyone in Cape Town knows him. You sure you don't know him?' she asked, peering at me from under hooded lids.

'No, I never heard of him,' I assured her.

'Jerry told us that all his top teeth are gold, studded with diamonds and rubies. Must be some glittering smile he has,' she remarked. 'Anyway he's still after them. I don't know what happens to these young men. He used to be a real angel, that one. You couldn't find a better child anywhere in these parts. Now he's always in trouble with the law.'

I shook my head sympathetically. 'They grow up too fast these days,' I agreed. 'He was about fourteen when I saw him last. Tall, skinny boy with pimples and big ears.'

36

'*Ja*. Like you were when you were sixteen,' she chuckled.

'I saw Marietjie the other day, she looked okay.'

Ousis shook her head. 'Poor thing,' she said tapping her head. 'She went a little strange. She still thinks she can see the future. I don't abide much by that nonsense, but others do. It's the devil's work.'

I grinned at Ousis's vehement scepticism. I knew that they all went to Marietjie to have their fortunes read. Everyone in the quarters went to her for advice. Some wanted to know whose baby their wife was carrying while others went to her to find out who their husbands were running around with. 'Whatever happened to Baba?' I asked.

Ousis shook her head. 'You thought your daddy was bad, but I tell you they don't come no meaner than Baba Jansen. Do you remember how he used to beat Marietjie and call her all sorts of names? He was always telling her that she was the ugliest thing this side of hell. This went on for years. Now how can anyone stand that all the time, I ask you? Well she did, but Jerry couldn't take it; that's why he ran off to Cape Town just like you.'

'I didn't know he was in Cape Town.'

'I thought your mama would have told you.'

I shrugged. Mama might have. I couldn't remember her saying anything about it, but then there had been so much on my mind lately.

A group of people passed by the house, nodding in our direction. They smiled timidly and shuffled by slowly and hesitantly, waiting for an invitation to drop in. Ousis ignored them and they walked on still smiling and nodding. I thought of the heat, the cold, the work, the hunger, the feeling of desperation behind all the small smiles and I knew that it was wrong of me to condemn them. After all, I was now the outsider.

'Someone's coming,' Ousis said coming upright and pointing into the distance.

I followed the direction of her hand but I couldn't see anything.

'You'll see them in a moment,' she said.

I peered down the road to where a cloud of dust had been churned up, then a blue van appeared.

'Oh, Lord, it's the police again,' Ousis said panicking. 'What is it now, *tog*?' she asked.

'Do they come often?'

She raised a shoulder. 'One is Constable Le Roux. He always comes around,' Ousis said, standing in the middle of the road. I had to yank her out of the way of the van which pulled up in a spray of sand and gravel. There were two white policemen sitting in the front and an African constable in the back.

'*Wel, wel, wat het ons hier?*' the white policeman in the passenger seat asked, his gaze flickering over me.

I presumed correctly that this was Constable Le Roux, and for the first time in many years I again felt the discomfort of being subjected to a white man's scrutiny. Without taking his eyes off me, he opened the door and stepped out. He was short and stocky and for a moment I was reminded of Koos Kleinhans. I even expected him to address me as '*hotnot*'.

It was like a spectre from my past; the policeman confronted me and I boldly met his gaze. With that uncanny sense that people have of trouble brewing, the others gathered around in a semi-circle. They gazed at the white Constable, some of them nervously, some boldly. The flat grey eyes of Constable Le Roux stared back from under his dark brows.

'Where you from?' he asked. His eyes slowly moving from the top of my head to the tips of my dusty shoes.

'Cape Town,' I said, trying to sound nonchalant.

'Cape Town, hey?'

He walked around me, his *sjambok* tapping the side of his leg. 'What you doing here?'

'I'm visiting my mother.'

'What's your mother's name?'

'Naomi Jacobs.'

'The son of Simon Jacobs, hey?' Le Roux sneered. 'Your father is a jail-bird. He's out now, but they should have hanged the bastard. He's a real mean son-of-a-bitch.'

38

After several unsuccessful attempts to intimidate me, he retreated to the van to seek counsel from his partner. They conversed in low tones while we waited. The rest of the curious onlookers, pressed in on us.

Le Roux returned. 'When last have you seen that *donder*, Baba Jansen?'

I ignored him.

'I'm asking you,' he snarled, pointing a finger at me.

I gazed at him steadfastly while he glowered back. He was so close to me that I could smell his foul breath. Then he leered at me through two grey slits. 'You bugger. I'm talking to you.'

Ousis nudged me.

'Look, I know my rights. I'm not some pumpkin picked out of the *veld*.'

'You just answer my focking question. That mother-focker got drunk and beat up a white man in town.'

I didn't say anything but felt a thrill of satisfaction as if Baba had done something that I had always wanted to do but had lacked the courage.

The others muttered and shook their heads, anticipating trouble.

But the policeman's attention was focused on me. 'I'm not taking any cheek from you, so you better watch out,' he hissed angrily. '*Nou, ja*,' he said returning to the business at hand. 'I'm asking you again. Any of you seen Baba Jansen?'

Silence once more.

He hoisted his pants and resting his hands on his hips, his glance slid around the group. 'You're a *verdomde nasie*,' he said. 'What about your father, Simon?' he asked me.

'Why do you want to know about Simon?' asked Ousis.

'We know he's somewhere around here. Maybe Baba is hiding out with him.'

I laughed out aloud.

'So you think that is funny, hey?' the policeman asked.

I turned away from him. He obviously didn't know Baba.

Ousis's hand fastened on my arm like a vice. She shook her head.

'They're not here, *Baas*,' a querulous voice piped up.

Le Roux's glance leaped from one face to the other, searching for the owner of that voice. It was Willem. He was the one who had told me all those years ago to say, '*Ja Baas*' to Kleinhans.

'What do you know about this?' Le Roux demanded.

'Nothing, I swear it. But you know how it is,' Willem said, giving Le Roux a toothless grin.

'No, I don't know how it is. You tell me.' He took his notepad from his pocket and with a flourish pulled the top off his ballpoint.

All eyes were on Willem who abruptly fell silent.

Le Roux waited, but he knew that he would get nothing more out of Willem.

He jammed the cap back onto his ballpoint and returned the pad and pen to his pocket. 'You'd better watch your step. I'll be back,' snarled Le Roux.

The policeman climbed into the van and with a parting scowl instructed his partner to swing around in the clearing. They left as they had arrived, in a cloud of dust.

'I wonder if it could be true about your daddy and Baba being together,' Ousis said.

'Could you think of two people better suited for each other. They've even committed the same crime,' I said. The irony had not escaped me.

'You don't know everything about it. I wonder why the police haven't thought of looking around the old shack yet. Le Roux can't be too smart hey?'

'It won't be long before someone tells them,' I said loudly, giving Willem a significant glance.

'You could take your mama to see your daddy. If Baba's there you can warn him that the police are looking for him.'

'Why should I?' I demanded.

'Because he's Marietjie's husband and whether you like it or not, he's one of us.'

The group of people dispersed and Ousis walked ahead. I followed her slowly, my hands clasped behind my back.

'They'll be back again,' she told me.

When I got back to the house Mama was waiting for me. 'Horace, there you are. Thank God,' she cried.

'What's the matter?' I asked, hurrying over to where Mama stood on the *stoep*.

'I fell asleep on the sofa,' she said, breathless with agitation.

'I know. I was outside talking to Ousis and then the police came ...'

'Son, I want you to take me to the shack right now.'

'Now?'

'I had this dream. It was a terrible dream. I have to see your daddy. Let's go!'

'Okay. Okay Mama. Calm down. I'll take you. Let me get the keys.' I hurried indoors, calling for Kenny.

'Can I come?' he asked.

'No, you wait here.'

'I always have to wait here,' he complained.

'Let him come,' Mama said impatiently.

'Come Gimpie,' he called.

'Leave the damn dog,' I snapped.

But the dog ignored me, and in one bound almost bowling Kenny over, he was in the back, panting excitedly.

'Never mind the dog, let's just go,' Mama said.

I opened the car for my mother and then got in. We drove most of the way to the shack in silence. Mama agitatedly folded and unfolded the hem of her shawl. Occasionally Gimpie barked and in between times Kenny plied me with questions.

I ignored him and spoke to Mama. 'What was the dream?' I asked curiously.

She drew a deep shuddering breath, shook her head and continued to stare out through her side window.

'We don't have too much further to go,' I said, turning off onto the dirt track. She held onto the dashboard as we bumped over the ruts.

'Where are we going?' Kenny whined.

'We're going to see your grandfather,' Mama said.

41

'Why are we going to the shack?'

'There it is,' she said.

I pulled up at the side of the shack. Mama opened her door and then hesitated.

'It doesn't look like he's home,' I said.

Kenny opened the door and Gimpie leaped out, barking furiously.

'What's that smell?' Mama asked.

'I don't know.'

'Something's wrong, Horace.'

Gimpie bounded to the door and rushed back again.

'Put that dog in the car,' Mama told Kenny.

It was quite a struggle but he finally subdued Gimpie and shut him into the car. Before I could stop him Kenny followed us into the shack. Baba was lying on his back on a crust of dried, flaking blood. The small gaping hole at the side of his head crawled with maggots and flies. The stench almost bowled us over. I rushed out for a breath of air, dragging Kenny outside with me. I instructed him to stay outside and returned to get Mama who was standing with the corner of her shawl cupped over her mouth and nose.

Thousands of flies swarmed everywhere, buzzing around the body on the floor. They were crawling over Baba's face, massing between his parted lips and on his staring eyes. Mama shooed the flies off his body with one hand, while the other kept her nose and mouth covered. Finally she took off her shawl and covered his face. I took her arm and led her outside.

'Thank God,' she said. 'It's not your daddy. Where could he be?' She paused a little guiltily at having expressed relief at someone else's misfortune. 'He's long dead; we'll have to bury him right away.'

I nodded.

'I'll help you,' she said.

'No. I'll see to it. But first I'll take you and Kenny home.'

She shook her head. 'You take Kenny home. Someone's got to stay here. We'll dig a hole right here beside the old shack,' she said pointing to a spot beneath a cypress tree.

'Mama I have to go back to the house. I don't have a spade and there's nothing here that I can use.'

'Okay. I'll wait here. Bring Ousis and Marietjie. Maybe together we can close his eyes ... and bring some sheets and lime. Ask Jaapie to help you.'

'Will you be all right?'

'*Ja*, I'll be all right, son. I just can't help being relieved that it's not your daddy lying there. But I just wonder who killed Baba. Could it have been your daddy?'

FIVE

Kenny was unusually subdued. He remained indoors all day even though Jannie had called on him, full of boyish eagerness for the grim details. Now after Jannie had gone, I could hear my son moving about inside. Out on the *stoep* Mama and I were both a little concerned about him.

It was an unseasonably warm evening. The silence was broken only by the chirruping of the crickets and the occasional distant howl of a dog or a jackal, which made Gimpie, who was lying beside Mama's rocker stop snoring, perk up his ears and without moving his head, roll his eyes from side to side.

Mama was silent, rocking back and forth, staring out into the gathering darkness. She sighed. 'I just wonder where he could be. He could never have killed Baba. Not like that with a gun and a bullet through the head. In the old days, yes, your daddy could have killed a man with his bare fists. This is not like him. He doesn't even know anything about guns.'

I was reluctant to admit that she was probably right. I was familiar with my father's temper, but this was a little far-fetched for the frail old man I had seen on the road the other day. I sat in contemplative silence feeling inadequate because I couldn't bring myself to offer the reassurance she needed. I wondered how Sissie would have reacted had she been here. Perhaps I should ask Celia to come? I mused. She would know how to comfort Mama.

'You'll never understand, Horace. What harm can he do now? He's a crippled old man. He spent eighteen years of his life in jail. Don't you suppose he's had enough time to think about what he's done to us?' She paused, studying me. 'Why do you think he came back to the valley? I know what he was going through. If there really is a Lord up there, I hope he can forgive us for being so uncharitable. Me, you and especially your sister who can run around forgiving other people, but who can't find it in her heart to forgive her own father. So much Christianity and the spirit that drove her to become a missionary.'

'What if he did kill Baba?' I asked.

'I know he didn't and so does Marietjie. She knows who the killer is.'

'What do you mean?' I asked in astonishment.

'I'm not saying another word. The truth will out.'

'Mama … ' I was aghast. 'If you know who the culprit is, it's up to you to speak up or the police will be running after the wrong man again.'

She sat there, back ramrod straight, wearing her *doek* partly over her forehead like a pirate in one of those old films.

We had already reported Baba's death to the police. They had told us that they would be there the next day to remove the body and to start the investigation. Mama said the only reason for the investigation was their anxiety to locate the gun that was originally stolen by Baba, and subsequently used in his murder.

'If you know who the killer is … ' I said.

Mama's lips clamped shut. The irregular thumping of her chair against the *stoep* was the only indication of her state of mind.

'I'll phone Celia to come and stay with you.' I spread my hands in a gesture of helplessness.

'I don't need nobody,' Mama replied sharply.

'I'll stay on for another week,' I said.

'Suit yourself.'

'Do you want me to read for you, *Ouma*?' Kenny asked, arriving on the scene with a book tucked under his arm.

'Not tonight, child, not tonight.'

I signalled Kenny with an inclination of my head. His face fell.

'Why don't you go over and play with Jannie for a while, then?' I asked.

'Don't be too late, though,' Mama added.

I sat outside with Mama until the sky was swallowed up in the inky-black vault of darkness. She shivered as the night air turned cold.

'Let's go inside,' I said. 'I'll light a fire in the stove.'

Mama followed me into the house. I could see she was worried that my father was out there somewhere on his own. 'Do you think you could take the car and go and find him?' she asked.

'How can I Mama? I don't have the faintest idea where he might be.'

The next morning I was up early. I hadn't slept and I suspected that Mama hadn't either. There was a thin layer of frost on the ground. I wore a heavy cardigan and sat out on the *stoep*, my hands wrapped around a mug of hot coffee. Mama joined me and I drew her chair out into the sun.

'Would you like a cup of coffee?' I asked.

'*Ja*, that would be nice.'

I went inside and returned with her chipped enamel mug half-filled with black coffee. We sat in silence sipping our drinks.

'It's strong coffee,' she remarked.

'I always make strong coffee.'

One of us will have to go over and talk to Marietjie.'

'I'll go, if you like,' I offered.

'*Ja*. Maybe that's a good idea. She may tell you the truth.'

'You seem to know about this. Why don't you tell me?' I asked.

'*She* has to tell you,' Mama said. 'I was thinking about Simon all of last night. I didn't sleep a wink.'

I turned my head and averted my glance.

'I know you don't want to talk about him,' she said, observing my obvious reluctance to discuss my father. 'I just want to make you understand that he isn't all bad. Your daddy had some good moments. That's why I married him. Once upon a time he was a sweet man. Kind-hearted like you wouldn't believe. But sometimes anger and frustration can make people do terrible things, especially if you can't see your life going anywhere. It was a terrible thing for Simon to be trapped here, owned like a slave by Andries van der Merwe. It was the same with Baba Jansen and the other men too. If you

46

hadn't left, you might have turned out the same way. I just wish I could show you what Simon was really like.'

'I know what he was like. I still have the scars to remind me.'

'What you don't understand, Horace, is that he hated everybody, but most of all he hated himself for what he was doing to us. It was like he was driven to hurt himself. You know yourself, it was always like he was burning up with a fever.'

'I only remember that he almost killed you.'

She shrugged. 'I forgave him for everything a long time ago. There's no bitterness or hatred left inside me any more.'

I listened in silence while Mama talked about a father who was not at all like the one I remembered. Why was it that we could perceive one person in two such completely different lights?

She went to lie down and I went for a walk to clear my mind. As I crossed the road I turned to look back at the house. Ousis said it would stand for ever. 'All the little boxes will be here long after we've gone,' she said. Most of the houses had been built more than a hundred years ago when these places were still run by slaves. Our house was like all the others in the quarters. At one time it had been nothing more than a windowless box, dark and dank with more than a century's history carved out on the stone walls. Before we fixed it up, the roof had consisted of a mixture of thatch and corrugated iron. From miles away you could hear the rain coming, drumming its way across the roofs like a herd of stampeding horses. After all these years the compound was still referred to as the 'coloured quarters' or 'slave quarters'.

The layers of whitewash on the other houses had flaked away and the small chimneys above the stoves had crumbled and collapsed from rot. Most of the houses leaked. One could smell the dampness; in winter the wind whistled through the cracks in the walls.

In summer when there was no breeze, the hot windowless rooms echoed with the anguish of the slaves. As a child I often

47

used to lie awake at night wondering about them, imagining them chained together, simmering in the heat of these stone ovens. It was more comfortable to sleep outside in summer. Most of the *stoeps* were added on and were of wood. In some places the wood was so rotten that it had splintered and broken off, forming traps for the unwary. Some of the houses had small lean-tos made of clapboard or whatever else was available, anything that would keep the rain out.

A single tap, more or less in the middle of the quarters, served the whole community. Around the tap the grass was knee high and snakes often used to lie in the shade. The flowers grew wild, matted together so thickly that it was hard to tell where one began and the other ended. There were always stagnant pools from the dripping tap, and when the women went to collect water in buckets they'd have to lift their dresses and be careful where they stepped. Other bits and pieces of rubbish littered the area: cartons, empty tins, pieces of plastic; an old wagon wheel, a broken plough, part of an old yoke; several bones, some of them the jawbones of cattle, buried and dug up over and over again by the dogs.

I remember my father once standing on this spot, talking about how the house needed fixing. He wasn't too bad looking in his younger days, but dark complexioned, with kinky hair. His father was Xhosa and his mother coloured. At times I wondered if this was what had given him such a complex. It was ironical that we complained about racial prejudice and then turned round and practised it amongst ourselves. At that time Daddy was forty-two, but even then he seemed much older. It was as though whatever was eating him from inside was also affecting him on the outside. Already he was grey and stooped. Mama said it was arthritis setting in from working in the rain and damp weather. But Ousis said it was all his sins that he had to carry on his back.

He never did anything about the house. It remained in disrepair. We always talked about mending the roof or fixing the *stoep* where the floorboards had broken away. But there was too much to do. It required too much energy; energy which none of us could spare.

I saw my mother as she used to sit on the *stoep* years ago, brushing a weary hand across her eyes. I was always sad for her, knowing that Daddy would never improve her lot. She was so important in my life. How could I ever bear to lose her? I used to wonder.

I went to see Marietjie later that afternoon. She was sitting in an old wooden kitchen chair, the rattan inset on the back-rest had frayed and hung in loose threads which snagged ones clothes. She had seen me coming and for a brief moment there was a little spark of something undefinable in her face.

'Hello Horace.'

'Hello, Marietjie, how are you?'

She raised a shoulder. 'All right. How are you?' she asked.

'Not too bad under the circumstances.'

'How is your mama today?' she asked.

'She has good days and bad days. On her good days it's hard to believe that she's sick.'

'*Ja*, I thought she looked much better. She says the medicine from *Tante* Sinnah works.'

'I hope so. Marietjie,' I paused then, trying to muster conviction for my words of sympathy, 'I'm sorry about Baba.' My words had a hypocritical ring to them I thought. 'Mama thinks you know who killed him. Is that right?' I asked.

She remained silent.

I shrugged. 'Mama knows too, but she won't tell me, she says it's up to you.'

Her back straightened and her eyes clouded over.

'You've got to tell the police; if you don't they'll go after the wrong man. Mama's afraid that they might even kill my daddy and all for nothing.'

She lowered her glance. 'What difference does it make? He's an old man and he was no good, just like Baba.'

'That's not the point. Mama's worried about him.'

She shook her head.

Watching her I wondered when there would ever be relief for communities like ours where lives were steeped in misery.

Her mind drifted away as if she had forgotten all about me, then after a long while she returned her attention to me. It was hard to believe that we were the same age because she looked like an old woman whose shoulders were stooped and bent under an invisible burden.

'There's always trouble,' she sighed. 'Baba's dead now, but there's still Jerry. I'm so tired of all the worries. Sometimes I just want to close my eyes and never wake up.'

I listened in silence thinking about what she had said. I couldn't help but feel sorry for her.

'I don't care that he's dead. I don't care how he died or who killed him,' she cried vehemently. 'He's dead and that's enough for me. If someone else didn't kill him, I might have.'

'You know who that *someone else* is, don't you?'

Although she ignored the question, an expression akin to panic flitted across her face and I knew then that Mama was right. It seemed that something was going on with Marietjie.

'Maybe now I'll have some peace and quiet.'

We lapsed into a long awkward silence and I realised that it would be best for me to go because she wasn't going to confide in me.

'There's still a lot more tragedy lying in wait for us all.' She rose so abruptly that her dress got caught on the back of the chair. For one brief moment as I leaned over to help her, our eyes met and I got an inkling of the depth of her despair.

'What is it, Marietjie?' I asked gently.

Before I could say anything more she turned and rushed into the house, slamming the door behind her.

I stood on the *stoep* for a long time, perplexedly staring at that closed door.

SIX

'Poor Marietjie,' Ousis said the next day when she came to see Mama.

'The police are all over the place,' I remarked.

'What won't be happening next?' asked Ousis. 'Only thing the police are worried about is the gun that killed Baba. They don't worry about us,' she said jabbing the air. 'Where are they when some husband chokes the life out of his wife, or locks his wife in the shed and sets it on fire? Where are they then?' she asked, her big bosom quivering with indignation.

The air here at *Driehoek* seemed to be filled with something sinister; something that would creep up on me when I least expected it. It hung in the air between the small dwellings, lingering in the windowless hovels like angry, resentful spirits.

Ousis and I sat in silence. She stared into the distance while I leaned forward, resting my head on my knees like I used to do when I was a child. I traced a pattern in the sand with a stick I'd picked up. My son came to sit beside me.

'How are you feeling today?' I asked him.

'Okay ... are the police going to catch *Oupa*?' he asked anxiously.

'Even if they catch him, there's nothing they can do to him; he didn't kill Baba,' I said.

Kenny's glance shifted to Ousis for confirmation.

'It was someone else,' I said, trying to reassure him.

'Who?'

'We don't know yet.'

'But we do have our suspicions,' Ousis said grandly. 'I know for sure Simon didn't do it. What would an old man like that go around killing people for? I always said Simon was a little touched in the head but I don't think he's that crazy.' She paused, shaking her head. 'You're damned if you do and you're damned if you don't. Funny thing about these men sometimes even when they don't want you, they don't want someone else to have you neither. In those days even though he beat Naomi, he would still be crazed with jealousy if

51

another man as much as looked at her. He swore that he'd cut her up so badly that no man would ever look at her again. That's when Sissie left for Swaziland.'

'Could he not have shot Baba in a fit of jealousy?' I asked.

'You saw him yourself,' she shook her head and paused reflectively. We were silent for a while. 'I wish you'd stay on a little longer,' she said suddenly.

'I've thought of that and I may be staying on for another week, no longer than that. Kenny and I both have to get back to school. I'll have to invigilate examinations and mark papers soon.'

Ousis removed the hatpin and clenched it between her teeth; then she took her hat off, stuck the pin amongst the violets and used the hat to fan herself. 'We have a school here too,' she said, fixing me with one of her direct glances.

'Forget it Ousis, you know I'm not coming back here to live,' I replied, a little put out by her persistence.

'I don't know anything of the sort. Your place is here. Look what's happening to the young people because there's no one to make sure they have a proper education.'

'I've given up hope for these people.'

'These people are your people too. This, my boy, is our heritage whether you like it or not. Our parents and grandparents lived and died here in these *pondokkies*. It's all very well for you not to care anymore. You've become too grand now for these humble beginnings.' She fell into an angry silence, the hat fluttering like the wings of an agitated butterfly.

I went to bed early on Friday night after making the necessary phone calls and arrangements to stay on for an extra week. I had thought of sending Kenny back by train but he wouldn't go; so I telephoned Celia to get in touch with his school in order to advise them that he was going to be a week late as well.

Except for the occasional sounds from outside, everything was very still and quiet. I couldn't sleep. I heard Mama coughing and realised that she was also having problems getting to sleep. Hours later I was still lying there wide-eyed, staring at the ceiling. Frustrated, I eventually got out of bed and quietly went into the kitchen. It was warmer here than in the bedrooms and I raked together the smouldering coals in the stove and threw in another log of wood. It sputtered into flames and I turned my back warming my buttocks and the backs of my legs. From where I stood I could see through the window. It was a dark, cold night, the moon and stars hidden behind a cover of cloud.

I was staring out into the vacant night, not thinking about anything in particular except of course the cold and my tiredness, when I thought I saw something move outside. Gimpie gave a low threatening growl and I went to the window. It was too dark to see anything outside. I waited though and when the cloud broke there was enough light from the moon for me to catch a glimpse of someone moving about. Very quietly I opened the door and crept out in my pyjamas. Except for the night sounds all was quiet.

I was about to turn back when I heard the sound of approaching vehicles. I stopped to listen. In the silence of the *veld*, sounds travelled great distances. It sounded like more than one vehicle and I hurried back into the house, lit the lamp and put on my trousers and shoes. I had just dressed when all hell broke loose outside with the screeching of tyres, the sounds of dogs barking, voices shouting, feet running across the gravel. Mama dragged on her old blue candlewick gown as she and Kenny rushed into the kitchen with Gimpie in tow.

'What's going on?' Mama cried.

'It's the police.'

'Who are they after?' she asked.

'I heard something outside, maybe it's Daddy.'

'Dear Mother in Heaven,' Mama exclaimed. 'See if you can find him Horace.'

We heard a loud pounding followed by the splintering of wood, accompanied by a confusion of voices and sounds coming from down the road.

'They're at Marietjie's,' Mama said. 'Put the lamp out Kenny.'

Kenny shut off the lamp and for a while we bumped around until our eyes became accustomed to the dark. From outside came sounds of boots pounding across the gravel on the road.

'There he is. He's heading for the vineyards,' someone cried.

There was a lot of cursing and swearing and I sensed Kenny's fear. 'You wait here with Gimpie,' I told him, holding onto the dog who was raring to go. 'Keep him locked up and you stay put.'

'Can't I come?' he asked Mama.

'No, you listen to your daddy,' Mama told him.

There was a knock at the door and before we could open it, Marietjie rushed in, clutching the front of her dressing-gown. For a moment she was illuminated in the headlights of a car and I saw her eyes wild and frightened. I remembered her words from the previous day about not caring that her husband was dead.

'What is it?' Mama asked. 'What's happening?'

'It's Jerry.'

'No,' I said. 'I think it's my father.'

She shook her head. 'It's Jerry, he was at home with me.'

'Marietjie, did Jerry kill Baba?' I asked.

She nodded. She couldn't speak. Gimpie growled and I raised my voice to shut him up.

'The police obviously know, too,' Mama said.

'You knew also, didn't you?' I said to Mama.

She nodded. 'Let's not argue about that now. Get the car.'

A policeman pushed into the house. 'Where is he?' he demanded.

'Where is who?' Mama asked calmly.

'The Jansen boy.'

'Do you see him here?' she asked.

'What are you doing here?' the policeman asked suddenly turning on Marietjie.

'It's none of your business what's she's doing here,' Mama interjected.

The policeman glared at Mama as he pushed past her to the bedrooms.

54

'He's gone down to the vineyards,' his partner called from the door.

The policeman rushed out and the two of them leaped into the van and sped off after their quarry.

'*Nou ja*, let's go.' But as I turned, Kenny was right behind me. 'Stay here,' I said, remembering how he had tagged after us the day we found Baba's body. I didn't want that incident repeated. It was too dangerous, anything could happen with all the police milling around. Gimpie was about to follow as well, but a loud scolding from me sent him scampering under the table.

'We can take the short cut,' I said waiting for Mama and Marietjie to get into the car. Then with a quick glance back to make sure that Kenny had gone into the house, I sped off, bumping over the track which led from the quarters to the vineyards.

About a mile further down we were stopped by a commotion of sorts where one of the police vans was stuck in the sand. Other police vehicles congregated and in a short while lights from all directions illuminated the scene. The dogs had picked up Jerry's scent and were barking excitedly.

'What are you doing?' I cried, leaping out of the car when I saw them readying their weapons.

'We've got him cornered,' a policeman said pointing ahead.

'He's only a boy,' I cried, shouting to make myself heard above the noise.

'*Oh, ja*,' one of them scoffed. 'Some boy he is to shoot his own father. You people are worse than animals.'

'Who's in charge here?' I demanded.

'So, it's the know-all school-teacher from Cape Town.' A familiar voice spoke up from behind me.

I turned into the face of Le Roux. 'If you harm that boy I'll see to it that you're held responsible.'

He gave me an incredulous look then burst out laughing.

'Let me talk to him, Le Roux. Let me bring him out. It's not necessary to kill him.'

'Constable Le Roux to you, *kerel*, and this is a police matter. All of you get the hell out of here.'

He grabbed my arm. I jerked free. At that moment I came dangerously close to punching him.

'Who is this?' an authoritative voice enquired.

'Some *jong* from Cape Town who thinks he knows too much.'

I peered into the darkness and a face became visible. 'I'm Horace Jacobs. This is the boy's mother,' as I spoke I drew Marietjie into the circle of light.

Confused and frightened, Marietjie seemed to shrivel away from the attention and she might have collapsed had I not taken hold of her one arm and Mama of the other. 'I'm a school-teacher from Cape Town. I grew up on this farm. Give me a chance to talk to him,' I pleaded. 'The boy is frightened. I'll bring him here and you can see for yourself that he's quite harmless.'

The man in charge thought for a moment then nodded. 'All right. But *pasop*. He has a gun.'

'Lord have mercy on his soul,' Marietjie sobbed.

Many of the people from the quarters had hopped onto the back of Stompie's lorry and were now huddled in small frightened groups. I thought I recognised Gimpie's bark, but at that moment I was too distracted at what was happening to pay attention to other things.

'Look after her,' I said to Mama and Ousis, helping Marietjie to the ground. 'I'll find Jerry, don't worry.'

'Kenny what are you doing here?' Mama cried.

I glanced around and there were Kenny and Gimpie. 'Dammit! Didn't I tell you to stay at home?'

'We came with Stompie.'

'Didn't I tell you … ?'

'It's all right,' Mama said, 'I'll see that he stays here.'

'You don't move from here,' I warned him.

'Be careful,' Ousis urged.

Cautiously I made my way down the path furthest from the lights. About four-hundred yards into the darkness I heard a rustle from the trees to my right. 'Jerry is that you?' I asked.

'*Ja.*'

I groped around. 'Where are you?'

'Over here,' he replied in a hoarse whisper. The cloud cover broke and I could see a dark form ahead of me.

I followed his voice and parted the bushes, thorns ripping my flesh. I peered into his face and I could see the whites of his eyes.

'Christ, Jerry! Give yourself up. The place is swarming with police.'

'Never! I'm not going into the slammer. The bastard deserved to die. He screwed up my life. They can kill me first hey. They can kill me.'

'They will. They've got guns,' I reminded him.

'I don't care, man. I'll take some of them with me. You see this,' he said, brandishing something under my nose.

I pushed his arm away. 'Don't be stupid!' I cried. 'Put that damn thing away.'

The lights from a passing van lit up the scene and for a moment his sardonic grin was illuminated. We stepped back out of sight.

'Don't you think your mother has gone through enough already? Make things easier on yourself, man.'

'Let them come after me. They'll be fucking sorry. Let the sons-of-bitches come! Let them come, I'll show them!' His voice was laced with hysteria.

'Hey you!' someone hailed through a speaker. 'What the hell's happening?'

Suddenly a dog barked, yelping wildly. It was Gimpie. The police Alsatians responded; more yapping and howling and then several dogs took off into the vineyard.

'Kenny, Kenny come back,' Mama shouted.

'Gimpie! Gimpie!' I heard Kenny's terrified scream, then more yapping from the dogs.

'Oh, Christ!' My heart almost stopped. I glanced up in horror realising what had happened.

'Oh, Jesus, please!' Mama cried.

In that instant, while my attention was diverted, there was a deafening crack beside my head.

I could still hear the dogs yapping. Everything seemed to take place in slow motion. I could pick out individual sounds and movements in the melee.

'Horace! Horace! It's Kenny!' Mama shouted.

'Don't shoot!' I screamed, rushing out into the open. More gunfire followed and without thinking I battened myself to the ground. There was some stumbling in the dark and a lot of cursing. I leapt up and then sprinted across to the other side. At that moment I had no thought or concern, other than the safety of my son.

'Don't shoot, please!' someone cried out. It sounded like Mama. I was convinced that it was the end for all of us. Finally there was a pause and in that lull I tore off to where I thought the sound of the dogs had come from, but they were silent now. 'Kenny! Kenny!' I called as I sprinted through the darkness. The shooting started again, something smashed into the tree behind me. The police were advancing, forming a dragnet.

Suddenly the lights from the police van illuminated the darkness. To my right were the dark forms of two constables. I slid over to the other side of the tree, hoping that Jerry had enough sense to lie low in the darkness. The van approached. A large searchlight flashed on and ahead in the open, Jerry was trapped in its beam like a jackrabbit.

There was a loud bang and he stumbled. In that moment I looked up and I saw his face clearly; his mouth agape, gulping air like a fish. His eyes were large and bewildered. My God, I thought, stunned. He's going to die.

I dashed out into the open, arms flapping wildly. 'Stop!' I shouted at the advancing policemen. But they continued on, revolvers at the ready.

Transfixed by the light, Jerry was crouched in the middle aisle between the rows of vines. He was hunched over, fingers on the ground like a runner awaiting a starter's signal. Then I saw him reaching into his pocket. It was so bright out with all the lights that I could actually see the point of the handkerchief as he drew it out of pocket, just as clearly as I saw the silvery thread of mucus dangling from his nose.

The two constables saw the movement, too. They saw him reaching into his pocket and in that instant one of them raised his gun. The bullet slapped Jerry in the head, pulling him upright and spinning him around like a dancer. The other policeman waited, gun aimed, ready to fire again. But nothing moved. I knew that it was all over.

I approached like a sleepwalker. The van came up behind me, Jerry was spotlighted in the beam of its headlights. He was lying face down, arms and legs splayed. A police officer placed his foot under Jerry's shoulder and turned him over. There was a dark stain on his forehead.

'Shit. A bull's eye, Malherbe. Right in the middle of the head. Good shooting Maat.'

'Jeez,' someone said in the darkness. 'He's only a boy.'

'That's the way it goes,' another responded. 'They're never too old or too young for trouble. You never know about these sons-of-bitches.'

'I thought he had a gun.'

'He did.'

'Where is it?' the first voice asked.

'We'll find it in the daylight,' another said.

'Daddy,' I turned at the sound of Kenny's voice. Dazed, I lifted my son into my arms, overcome with relief that he was all right. 'They killed Gimpie,' he sobbed.

'It's all right son. It's all right,' I soothed, turning him away from the sight of the body and the police. I noticed my father then, he was standing to one side. He didn't have to say a word, I knew merely by looking at him, that somehow he was responsible for getting Kenny back safely. We exchanged glances and as he was about to walk away, I said: 'Daddy, wait a moment. I want to thank you for getting Kenny out of trouble.'

He didn't say a word. He just stood there with the same quiet dignity with which he used to confront Koos Kleinhans. Then with a shrug of resignation, he left.

'Mama would like to speak to you,' I said. It was the least I could do.

But he continued on, hunched over his cane.

'*Oupa*,' Kenny called.

But it seemed that the old man hadn't heard either of us. Kenny and I watched until he was swallowed up in the darkness just beyond the periphery of the lights.

SEVEN

Jerry was buried on the following Thursday afternoon. The police were there too, not to pay their respects but to complete their investigation. Disregarding the solemnity of the occasion they poked around in the grass trying to find more evidence that Jerry had killed his father. We had all been questioned. I had been questioned several times and I suspected that it wasn't over for any of us yet.

'Can't they leave things alone now that both of them are dead?' Mama asked.

My father came to see Mama three times and on each occasion you couldn't pry Kenny away from his side. He and Mama had spent a lot of time talking and I knew that the moment I was gone, he'd be back home again. I still didn't have much to say to him but after the way he had saved Kenny I didn't feel quite as antagonistic towards him any more.

I studied him surreptitiously and noticed little things about him that I hadn't been aware of before. I could tell that he was someone who valued his solitude. Perhaps life in prison had had that effect on him. Mama discounted this, saying that he had always been a loner. I could see that she was a lot more at peace with herself. Their getting together might have been a happier occasion for her at least, had it not been for the tragic events of the past week. Instead of gathering for a celebration of life, we had again gathered to mourn the death of one of our own.

I felt self-conscious. I had this image of myself as a comic figure, incongruous in my city-bought patents and dark suit. I stood out amidst the black crepe dresses and ill-fitting trousers, shiny with wear. I don't think there was a more bedraggled and motley group of mourners than the one following the coffin to the foot of the mountain.

After the sermon the six of us stood by the grave, three on either side, each holding onto the end of a piece of rope, waiting for the minister's signal to lower the coffin to its final resting place.

Images of my childhood here at *Driehoek* came back to me, buffeting and pummelling me in a tide of memories. So little had changed since I left here all those years ago. Last night the wake took me back to those early days: the raised voices arguing drunkenly, the spilling of cheap wine and cheap tears, while out on the *stoep Outa* Jaapie coaxed the purest melodies out of his mouth-organ, and Auntie Ester's voice filled the valley with exquisite sweetness. But when the wine took over, the beat and rhythm of the hymns changed and it wasn't long before Fat Maria and Dora were stomping, swaying, and dragging their feet in the dust, eyes tightly shut in religious ecstasy.

Today, however, in the bright light of reality their expressions were sombre, their eyes red from crying and carrying on at the wake. The men, especially, were unusually withdrawn. Perhaps they were intimidated by the minister who blamed them for what had happened here.

The jerk of the rope abruptly jarred me back to the present. The coffin swayed dangerously, bumping against the walls of the grave as it slithered unchecked. Those of us on the end hauled up and the coffin tipped. We righted it and paused to mop the sweat from our faces.

Where is the justice? I wondered.

'Hold fast, man!' Willem grunted as the coffin tilted again.

'*Dis die verdomde tou.*' Arendse cursed, loudly blaming the near mishap on the rope supplied by Mannetjie.

The frayed rope looked like something that might once have been used on a fishing boat. In fact yesterday while we were struggling to undo the knots I caught the faint smell of fish and ocean.

'*Die tou is vrot.*' I had added my complaint last night to the growing litany of concerns that the rope might not hold the weight of the coffin.

'Don't worry, man. That *tou* will do the job,' Mannetjie had assured me. 'It can still pull a car.'

Daddy with Kenny and Jannie at his side, had sat through all the grousing and complaining, quietly listening. Eventually he and the boys went for a walk. I suspected that he was entertaining them with adventure stories, but none reflecting his own experiences, I thought cynically.

The rope and the problems constituted by it, took up my attention. It was knotted so firmly in places that we couldn't get the knots undone.

Everyone pitched in to help, all of them touched by the tragedy that had struck the Jansen family. The women all came with something they had prepared for the wake or the funeral, sharing the little that they had with each other. Some of them brought samp and beans, others had prepared tomato *bredies* with chunks of rabbit meat. Others had baked.

One woman brought a pot of *magou*, the mealie-meal forming little bubbles which fermented and burst like tiny pockets of boiling mud. The last time I had this drink was when Mama had made it. She always used to keep a small pot of soured mealie-meal porridge under the stove which she used as starter for a fresh batch of *magou*. Sometimes a mug of this gruel had as much kick in it as a bottle of cheap wine. Others brought wine made from stolen grapes. Ousis said it was the best kind. Better than the grandest Muscatel stored in the cellars of the winery here at *Driehoek*.

Mama had offered our house for the wake. It was a big gathering. The whole community was in attendance, others even came from the neighbouring farms. There were some people whom I hadn't seen in years, and with all the news and stories to exchange we lost track of how much liquour we had consumed.

Today of course we were paying the price. I noticed the dazed look on the faces around me. Dull eyes stared ahead, unfocused and fixed on a spot other than the gaping hole which reminded them of their own mortality. We struggled to right the coffin again. The knots hampered its progress. Finally when it reached the bottom, rather than struggle with the retrieval of the rope, we tossed it into the grave. I watched with a preoccupied air of grief as it snaked against the walls before collapsing in a coiled heap onto the coffin.

Ousis sniffed loudly and dabbed her eyes with her handkerchief. They were red rimmed and swollen from all the crying. Mama used to say that there was not another mourner who could hold a candle to Ousis, and last night at the wake she had shown her true form.

Ousis had lined the coffin with a piece of peach-coloured satin which she had saved for a more auspicious occasion. Auntie Helen came over bringing a pillow-slip she had embroidered at convent school more than fifty years ago. And so with bits and pieces put together Jerry's body was accorded some semblance of dignity. Lying in the coffin he could well have been asleep. The women had done a good job laying him out, despite the way he had been mutilated during the autopsy.

I frequently caught Mama glancing over at Daddy who was talking to some of the men out on the *stoep*.

Ousis stood up for Jerry at the wake and there wasn't a dry eye in the room. Marietjie sat beside Mama, quietly sobbing. In a deep, husky voice Ousis spoke of the boy whose life had ended much too soon. A needless and senseless death. Who was to blame?

'Gentle Jesus,' she murmered, 'bless this boy, Jerry Jansen.' She stood at the head of the coffin. With her arms raised, her head thrown back, and with the rolls of fat trembling, she struck a formidable pose.

'Amen,' everyone muttered.

'Dear Lord, in your mercifulness, I beseech you, forgive him. In his tormented and anguished state he sinned.' Her voice crept up, spreading into all the dark and dank crannies.

There was a low murmur of 'Amen,' from the women squatting on the floor in the far corner.

'Yes, dear Jesus, he sinned! But he was a good boy, a good son, devoted to his mother. Deep down he was a good Christian.' Ousis's voice trembled in the high octaves.

Mama rolled her eyes at this reference to a good Christian. She didn't abide by the dictates of the church. She said the church was like a stage for all the world's biggest sinners.

Drinking and fornicating on Friday, then staggering home drunk on Saturday to beat their wives and children. Then after all that drinking, on Sunday the church throbbed with life, those very same sinners climbing the walls in religious fervour.

'We have all suffered and now we all stand here before you, O Lord, your servants, all of us sinners. Not one of us in this room can say: Lord we are better than Jerry Jansen.'

There was muttering from the Amen corner. A few stragglers hastily joined in the amening.

Ousis's voice became louder, more frenzied. Her big bosom shook and her finger punctuated the air. 'Lord he's standing before you!' Her eyes opened wide, sweeping the room, then they closed and she threw her head back, shouting: 'Hallelujah!'

'Hallelujah!' the others cried.

'Take him to your bosom, dear Lord, that he may have everlasting peace, free of suffering. For Christ our Lord's sake ... '

'Amen,' the others whispered, moved by Ousis's dedication.

'Amen,' I whispered.

'Amen,' Ousis Cook said. Then after a moment's silence, the mourners lifted their voices in the hymn:

> Rock of ages cleft for me,
> let me hide myself in thee
> let the water and the blood ...

The voices swelled with passion, the words plaintively rising. Against the vast background of darkness only the jewelled heavens responded with flickers of light.

The mound on his grave was decorated with wreaths woven from branches and vine leaves. Someone had filled a jar with wild flowers but in the heat they soon withered and died.

Three days later while playing out in the *veld*, Jannie and

Kenny found Marietjie's body. She had reached the end of her endurance and had hanged herself from a tree.

'Mama, I wish you would return to Cape Town with me,' I said on Sunday, the day after Marietjie's funeral.

Mama shook her head. 'No, this is where Simon and I will stay out the rest of our lives. When my turn comes, I want to be buried here amongst the others where I belong,' she said, adjusting her *doek*.

'Daddy can I stay with *Ouma* and *Oupa*?'

'No, son.'

'I want to say goodbye to *Oupa*.'

'All right.'

'How are things going between you and Daddy?' I asked when Kenny had gone.

'We have a lot to talk about and not much time in which to do it. We're two old bodies, trying to forget the past and go on with whatever is left of our future. Every moment we have now is like *bonsella*.'

'I suppose he'll be coming home?'

'Yes. It's getting too cold for him to be alone out there.'

'At least Sissie's coming home too,' I said.

Ma nodded. 'It'll be so nice to see her. I've been longing for her. I just hope she doesn't cause trouble with your daddy.'

On the day that Marietjie's body was found, Stompie had come over with a message that Sissie had telephoned Pik van der Merwe to say that she was arriving in Cape Town at the end of the month; it was already the fifteenth of the month. I was surprised that Pik should have taken the trouble to relay the message but then Sissie always had a lot of nerve. I expected that she was going to spend some time with me in Cape Town first before coming to *Driehoek*. It was just as well so that I could prepare her for everything. Perhaps she too had changed. I suspect that her work and her long absence from this place might have mellowed her a bit. We've all grown older.

I thought of Daddy and glanced over my shoulder to where he was standing. The place was very quiet without the dog. I was glad that Daddy had carried Kenny away before he could see how brutally Gimpie had been mangled by the jaws of the police dogs. We had buried his remains near the cemetery.

I sensed that Kenny also had changed in the past few weeks. I suppose it was to be expected, so much had happened. Kenny returned. Daddy still stood some distance away, almost as though he was reluctant to intrude. I went over. 'Goodbye,' I said awkwardly. I didn't offer my hand.

He nodded.

Mama waited for me and then walked with me to the car. Kenny waved at his grandfather and would have run off to him again had I not stopped him. It was getting late and we had to get away.

I watched him walking ahead of us to the car. He was still grieving for Gimpie, I could tell by the way he scuffed the ground with his shoes.

'Poor boy, his loss has made him grow up, too,' Mama said. 'It's been quite a tragic week for all of us.' Her head covered in its *doek* bobbed beside me. It was very quiet outside on this crisp winter day. In the silence I could hear every blade of grass stirring in the breeze that had sprung up.

Glancing around, I realised with a dreadful feeling of despair that I could never sever my ties with this place. Whenever I thought of home, it wasn't city lights but images of the open *veld*, the vineyards, the mountains, the brilliant sunsets and star-filled nights which came to mind. I knew that despite all the anguish this place held for me, that it would draw me back time and time again. I looked back. Daddy was still standing there – alone and apart – leaning on his cane, watching.

SOMETHING IN THE AIR

'By God, we'll get them both this time. You make bloody sure of it or so help me it'll be your head on the block!'

Her father's study door was slightly ajar on Sunday evening when Elsie heard his angry outburst. Startled she stopped midway up the stairs, her attention drawn by the sound of her father's voice raised in anger. She peered over the bannister but could not see into the study to identify her father's visitor. She dallied on the stairway, audaciously listening in on the rest of the conversation.

'Marais sent a message that Bezuidenhout will be crossing the border this Friday. Apparently the young Indian is very deeply involved in this whole scheme,' her father told his visitor.

'We only have five days, then,' a male voice replied.

'*Ja*. But we will be waiting for them right here,' her father said. 'If the worst comes to the worst ... shoot the *donders*, but remember one thing. I want Bezuidenhout alive.'

Her father, Faanie van Staaden, was not only the local sergeant of police but also worked with the Special Branch Forces involved in tracking down terrorists and political agitators who tried to make their way to and from the Botswana border a hundred miles to the north.

For Faanie van Staaden it was generally all the same – dead or alive. The one exception was in the case of Daan Bezuidenhout, a once respected Afrikaner lawyer who was at the top of the Special Branch's list of wanted men. Moscow trained, Bezuidenhout's speciality was urban terrorism. And Faanie wanted him alive.

'To think that the *coolie* grew up in town right under my nose

67

and I didn't know what he was up to,' her father said, almost unable to believe that he could have been so negligent.

He had never cared much for Indians and made no bones about it. In his estimation they were a treacherous bunch, too smart for their own good. 'The country would have been a lot better off had the government put them all back on a boat to India, in 1948,' he used to say.

Elsie crept up the stairs to her room. The word *coolie* brought back so many associations. She wondered if the Indian referred to in her father's conversation was the same one she had met when she was about eleven years old. A fuzzy image of a lanky boy with black hair came to mind and for a while, as she prepared for bed, she struggled to recall his name. Eventually just as she was dozing off it came to her.

On Tuesday morning Elsie reluctantly drove into town. Her father had taken the jeep and her mother's small car was quite inadequate for carrying a load of any kind. The only vehicle at her disposal, therefore, was the old *chorrie* lorry. Her father who generally brought home the supplies on a Monday afternoon was too busy to do so that week, and since Elsie was home from boarding school he instructed her to pick them up from Faurie's General Store in town. She would not have minded, had he not been so gruff and off-hand with her and her mother.

He was always too busy, she thought resentfully, as she climbed into the truck for the twenty-mile drive into town. Even when she was a child, she and her mother hardly ever went anywhere because even at that time her father was preoccupied with terrorists and troublemakers.

The town which was located close to one of the Bophuthat-swana territories and, not far beyond that, to Botswana, where many of the terrorists were given refuge, was of strategic importance. As a consequence Sergeant Faanie van Staaden enjoyed a prominent role in the community.

Jackson, one of the farm labourers, accompanied her to load the bags of flour, mealie-meal, samp, sugar and other supplies for the week. Instead of riding in the front with the *klein*

Missies, he stood in the back, choking on the dust kicked up behind them, hanging on for dear life as the lorry with its broken suspension bucked like a cantankerous old horse.

It was a slow, dusty ride along the ten miles of corrugated farm track. The old lorry strained to the top of each hill as though it would rattle to pieces. Eventually they reached the main road, much of which had been tarred to facilitate the movement of troops all the way to the border.

Crawling along at a snail's pace, Elsie's mind meandered all over the place, but her thoughts returned to the Indian boy, on her mind so much since Sunday when she had overheard her father's conversation. She recalled when they met during that school break about ten years ago. She was about eleven and the boy, Rashid, about fifteen.

The schools had closed on a Friday and normally by Monday she was already bored silly. At that time they still lived in the *dorp*. It was the period just before her father bought the farm, *Vreugde*. Life became a little more interesting when they moved to the farm but she always retained the same dread of Sundays.

On the *dorp* they were boring lethargic days, waiting for something interesting to happen, a futile expectation in those days because the children were not to be seen or heard while the adults took their afternoon nap. Afterwards when the adults awakened, the children had to sit quietly on the *stoep* listening to the drone of voices while the grown-ups discussed the two popular subjects of the day: farming and politics.

She was always thankful when Sundays were over; wished away in the hope that Monday would present better possibilities. She remembered how she had lazed around the house on that first Monday morning of the school holidays ten years ago, driving her mother to distraction with all her questions. Finally in the afternoon when Sinnah van Staaden could no longer stand having her daughter underfoot, she told her to play outside.

Encouraged by her mother, Elsie went off that afternoon in search of adventure. At the far end of town her feet automatically turned towards the river, following the path-way along the bank; poking at the clumps of bushes with her stick because the one thing she dreaded most was coming unexpectedly upon a snake.

Eventually Elsie arrived at the old weir. At first glance it appeared to be deserted. Disappointed she was about to turn back when she spotted the tall, lanky, youth. He was fishing, his bare feet planted on a smooth river stone, trousers rolled up below his knee, exposing dark, roughened calves. On the rock beside him was a small plastic pail.

Fishing was not one of her favourite pastimes. It was boring to wait around for some dumb fish to bite, and the thought of squeezing a worm onto a hook filled her with revulsion. She watched idly. There was an air of aloof detachment about him like someone who had built a wall between himself and the rest of the world. He did not see her until she was standing right beside him.

'What are you doing here?' she demanded sharply. This was her spot and she was resentful of the invasion by this stranger.

Startled, he almost lost his balance. His dark eyes, reddened by the sun, glanced down at her in irritation.

Her eyes as she watched him, were full of frank curiosity. 'Who are you?' she asked. Then before he could answer she demanded: 'What are you doing here?'

He tilted his head slightly and with an indulgent smile, as though speaking to a child, replied: 'My name is Rashid. I'm fishing, can't you see?'

The condescension in his tone made her retract the friendship she had so cautiously offered. 'I know you're fishing. Do you think I'm stupid or something?' she snapped, using the same tone with which her father addressed the Blacks. 'Where do you come from?'

He inclined his head towards town.

'Are you from the *coolie* shop?'

At first he was taken aback then he laughed at her insolence. But when he discovered an absence of malice in her expression

70

he began to understand something his mother had told him one day when he came home angry and indignant about being insulted by one of the Afrikaners in town.

'They're ignorant, Rashid, sometimes they're like frightened little children. Leave them alone. They don't know any better. We mustn't get mad, we must teach them the right way. Show them that we are even better than them,' his mother said.

'What's so funny?' asked Elsie, offended by his laughter.

'You are. You *Boere* are so ignorant.'

'Don't you call me a *Boer*!' she cried stamping her foot.

'Well don't go around calling me a *coolie*.'

'But you are one,' she said in a small voice, a little unsure of herself now.

'No,' he said. 'It's a bad word.'

The wind had come up, rippling the calm surface of the water, sweeping her hair across her face so that it got into her mouth and made her sputter.

'You don't call me *coolie* and I won't call you *Boer*. Is that a deal?'

She studied him for a moment, her dark blue eyes intelligently considering his proposition. Finally she offered her silence as tacit agreement, and asked instead: 'What kind of fish have you caught?'

He grinned and shrugged. 'I don't know what they're called. They're just fish,' he said, reaching into the bucket and bringing out a small, flat silver fish which he offered to her in the palm of his land. 'Lots of bones though. My mother doesn't like them because of that.'

The wind died down again and for a moment he concentrated on his fishing. She stood a little to the side and behind him, watching him reel in the fish.

'You eat lots of carrots, hey?' he teased, turning his head slightly to glance at her over his shoulder.

'What do you mean?' she demanded, her brows coming together defensively. But she knew what he meant. Everyone teased her about her hair.

71

'Your red hair,' he grinned.

Elsie resented his remark. He was being forward and she didn't like that. She wanted to hurt him with words of her own and when none came to mind, except *that* word, she retreated, marching off in a huff.

But the next day she returned again. He was there. Every day of that week Elsie stopped by the old weir, and on each occasion she learnt a little more about him. He told her that he was at school in Jo'burg and that like her, he too was on holiday.

During the first few days she stood on a rock behind him peering over his shoulder while he fished, stepping back as he cast his line into the deep end; then with her hands carefully clasped behind her back, closing in to share the excitement when he had a bite.

Sometimes while they waited she prattled on, asking many questions. The knowledge that he was an outsider who had come home for the holidays, created a bond of sorts between them. The fact that he was Indian seemed of no further consequence and in the ensuing days no reference was made to either of the offensive words.

He spoke hesitantly about his family and she told him a little about hers. She discovered that they were both *only* children, his older brother having died several years before. Being an only child was one more thing that they had in common. He told her that their house was behind the store.

Elsie confessed that she had never been to the store.

'You should come one day,' he said.

Elsie slowed down to avoid a large bump in the road where the tar had heaved up and remembered so clearly the good feeling she had had at the end of that week when she and Rashid had become firm friends. It had nothing to do with the fact that she'd had no one to play with because all her friends had gone away for the holidays.

On the following Monday when she returned to *their* spot, he was not there. Thinking that he might have been delayed,

72

she waited and when he still did not come, she went looking for him at the store. She did not go in though. Instead she peered through the window, catching a glimpse of his parents. But of him there was no sign.

On the following Wednesday, after having gone to their spot on three successive days without finding him, she returned to the store. This time she went inside on the pretext of buying some sweets. His mother was there, dressed in a yellow sari.

There was a peculiar odour that drifted into the shop from the house. The smell of spices and sandalwood was unfamiliar to her. How could she have known that it was the smell of curry and incense?

'Where's Raasit?' she asked his mother, after she had made her small purchase.

His mother smiled, amused by her question. 'Rashid has gone back to school, my dear,' she said.

That was the last time Elsie had gone into the store. The following year her father had bought the farm, *Vreugde*, twenty miles out of town and she was shipped off to boarding school. She had not seen or heard anything further about him until the day she overheard her father's conversation.

Near the town the sun-baked earth changed to fields of bleached grass and stalks. She hit a pot-hole in the road and the lorry bounced on its worn springs. The jar drove her head against the roof, she cursed loudly and slowed down.

Peering into the mirror, she saw that Jackson, who had been standing up against the cab, had not fared too well either.

'*Stadig, klein Missies!* Slow down!' he cried, thumping the roof of the cab. Fortunately he had braced himself against the safety-bar in the back of the lorry, and after being bounced into the air had landed on his feet, slightly winded but unhurt.

Elsie reached the outskirts of the town. Then on a sudden impulse turned off onto the backroad which passed by the Indian store. It was still there just as she remembered it; the little snub-nosed building set back from a sandy road. The same blue sign proclaiming 'G.M. Trading Co.' hung from the side, a little more battered than it used to be. She wondered as she saw this what the initials G.M. stood for.

The ground in the front of the building was worn smooth; so was a footpath which cut across a field of mealies to the location. The heat had bubbled the paint which had cracked and peeled away exposing the many layers beneath.

Chained to the bars of the long window which almost reached the ground, were several metal trunks of the variety commonly used by African travellers. Beside the entrance to the store was a stack of three-legged iron pots used for cooking in the open. Bunches of billy cans hung from the door like Christmas decorations.

An assortment of metal signs were stuck to the outside walls like postage stamps, each advertising a product. One of these signs showed a cheerful black face holding up a bottle of Coca Cola; another, an African man with glossy hair proffering a tin of pomade. Directly below this was another sign with a picture of a contented baby, its well-being attributed to the tin of Lactogen in the foreground. At the far side was yet another sign with the picture of a light-skinned African woman who had placed her trust in a jar of Metamaphosa cream.

Elsie drove by slowly straining to peer inside, but the merchandise hanging from the doorway obscured her view. She brought the old lorry to a shuddering halt about three hundred yards past the store then carefully backed up to the door.

'Wait here,' she told Jackson as she lowered her sandalled feet to the ground.

In the store two counters at right angles demarcated the public area. It seemed that little had changed since the time she had stopped here in search of Rashid. A few cheap watches waiting to find a new home, lay face upwards on the top shelf in the glass display case. Behind this counter was a clutter of merchandise thrust haphazardly into the shelf space. The other counter contained sweets and jars of colourful beads.

Elsie recognised Rashid's mother. Although her face was

still relatively smooth and unlined, her black hair was peppered with grey. The yellow sari looked familiar too, perhaps a little faded, the frayed fringe forming balls of tangled thread.

For a moment she wondered what Rashid had done after leaving school. She was almost tempted to ask his mother but changed her mind. She remembered him telling her that he needed to be free of the small town and all the restraints it held for him. Johannesburg was where 'it' was happening. Years later, when she was in high school, she discovered what he had meant by 'it'.

The woman watched her, a little suspiciously at first. Elsie could see her hesitation, could see that she expected her to retreat. But instead of hurrying away, Elsie dallied, examining the contents of the showcase, trying to decide how she would respond to the woman's questions.

Ayesha Moola surreptitiously studied the newcomer. There was something vaguely familiar about the girl's face, especially the red hair, but at that moment she couldn't place her. Ayesha adjusted the sari over her shoulder. The corner of her mouth twitched into a half-smile as her glance settled on the young woman. Because it was not usual for Whites to wander into the store, a dozen speculative thoughts ran through her mind. Amidst these an alarm went off.

Ayesha knew only that her son was participating in a dangerous mission which involved the fugitive, Daan Bezuidenhout. The mere thought of the danger he faced filled her with dread. So many freedom fighters had been killed by the police in this area. It was too dangerous. When her son had visited the previous week, she had begged him not to go. Finally when all else failed, she had offered some unsolicited advice, albeit in a circumspect manner.

'You know, Rashid,' she said. 'If I were going to smuggle someone important across the border, someone like a white person for instance, I would put some brown stuff on his face and tie a turban around his head like a Sikh. That way I could say he was my father's brother, or something like that, you know.'

Rashid said nothing. Not a word of denial or approval or anything like that. All he did was exchange glances with his father.

The next day with heavy heart, she had watched him getting into his car for the drive back to Johannesburg.

'What do they know about the difference between a Sikh, Moslem or Hindu? What do you think, hey Goolam?' she had asked her husband over breakfast that same morning, her glass bangles jangling as she gestured with her hands.

Goolam had merely shrugged and had continued with his breakfast, but she could see that he too was full of anxiety.

There was something in the air. Ayesha could feel it. It was nothing she could articulate, just a vague nagging premonition which had put her on edge.

She studied the white girl. Perhaps it was the duplicating machine. Could it be that someone knew about the machine concealed behind a panel in the kitchen wall?

The Afrikaners in town didn't worry much with them and so sometimes people from the 'Congress'* would come and go without raising suspicion; but lately the police had been watching the store and asking questions. It was a big worry for her and it also made for a lonely life because the others had been warned to stay away. Now no one came any more and it was strange for her not to be cooking and entertaining a steady stream of people.

'Good morning,' Elsie said in Afrikaans. She smiled a little nervously, as she began to realise that it was a silly idea to have come here. Why should she care about them? Rashid was probably one of those who laid land mines which killed innocent people. In her opinion they deserved what they got. But it was a little difficult to envisage the young boy with his dark laughing eyes cast in such a ghastly role.

Ayesha still uneasy, was relieved when at that moment her husband entered the store through the side door. He came to

*African National Congress (ANC).

an abrupt halt in the doorway when his glance alighted on Elsie.

In a quiet, even voice with one brow arched, he addressed his wife in Gujarati. She responded in the same language. He smiled at Elsie.

'Good morning,' Elsie said.

'Good morning,' Goolam replied. Still smiling he made a comment to his wife in Gujarati again. The smile never left his face as he peered short-sightedly at Elsie. He was short, robust and balding. The shirt buttons were straining to contain the excessive bulge of his belly which ballooned over his belt.

'You must be the new lady teacher in town,' he said.

Elsie did not reply. Instead her glance was drawn to the two large curry stains on his shirt. He waited, but she gave no explanation.

'I was just saying to Abdul,' Ayesha spoke up, 'you look so familiar.' She paused, studying Elsie. 'Doesn't she look familiar Goolam? Who are you, my dear?'

'My name is Elsie and I am on holiday,' she muttered, her tone discouraging any further questions.

'Oh,' Ayesha said, lapsing into awkward silence.

She had a smooth round face with dark eyes which were strangely haunting. The pendant hanging from a gold chain was trapped in the cleavage of her full breasts, thrust up voluptuously by the tight, white calico bodice she wore beneath her sari. When she raised an arm to adjust the fold of sari on her shoulder, her glass bracelets clinked against each other.

'My wife must be mistaken. You know, she was just telling me she remembers a young girl with your hair colour coming into the shop a long time ago. Sometimes, you know, our memories are not what they ought to be. Huh, Ayesha?' he ventured, breaking the silence and giving his wife an affectionate grin.

'I was so sure, Goolam. But you are right. I must be mistaken.' Her hands flicked in gestures while she spoke, the steady clink of her bracelets punctuating her words.

She placed her hands on her hips and studied Elsie, the elusive memory struggling to surface. Her dark intelligent eyes flicked back and forth, not wishing to offend the white woman again by being too direct.

'I want to buy some of my supplies from you,' Elsie said.

'I thought you were on holiday,' Ayesha said with alacrity.

'It's not for me.'

'I'm just asking because the white people don't buy from us. They go to Faurie's,' Ayesha continued, exchanging glances with her husband.

'Ayesha, my dear. We must not look a gift-horse in the mouth. The lady must have her reasons for not wanting to patronise Faurie's,' he said, glancing at Elsie for confirmation.

Elsie nodded.

'Who did you say you were visiting?' Ayesha asked.

'I didn't.'

'Oh,' Ayesha said flustered, distractedly moving the watches around on the top shelf in the showcase.

'I need two bags of flour, a bag of mealie-meal ... '

'Do you have a list?' Goolam smiled apologetically for interrupting.

'Here it is,' Elsie said, handing it to him.

He passed the list to his wife who expertly scanned it. 'We'll have it ready for you in a jiffy. Would you like a cool drink?' she asked. Although she was polite there was an aloofness about her, born of her earlier suspicions.

Elsie nodded. 'I'd like that ... You could add it to my list and also one for Jackson. He's sitting in the lorry.'

'Of course. We'll call him in,' Ayesha said, directing the comment at her husband, who went outside.

Goolam returned with Jackson who stood to one side, nervously wringing his cap. Ayesha's smile, however, as she handed him the cool drink was reassuring.

'You can sit down on this chair if you like,' she said to Elsie.

'Don't worry about me,' Elsie replied. 'I'll take a look around.'

When the supplies were ready, Goolam helped Jackson to

load the lorry while Elsie settled the bill with Ayesha.

'I hope you'll come again,' Ayesha said as Elsie prepared to take her leave.

'I will.' She sniffed. 'What is that smell?' she asked curiously.

Ayesha's eyes widened in amusement. 'Curry,' she said. 'That's what we eat. It's really very good, you should try it sometime.'

'I don't know much about it,' Elsie protested.

'The next time you come in, maybe you'll want to try some. What do you think Goolam?' She smiled at her husband and turned her attention back to Elsie. 'Let me know. Are you coming in at the same time next week? I'll cook *roti* as well and you can sample a little bit of India,' she called gaily. Ayesha was a different person; quite buoyant now that she had shed her earlier reservations.

'Thank you,' Elsie said.

'Come again,' Ayesha called from the doorway.

Elsie climbed into the lorry and started the engine.

'What a lovely young girl. Who was she, Goolam?' Ayesha asked, returning to the store.

'Faanie van Staaden's daughter,' he said.

'How do you know that, Goolam?' she asked, her voice thin and quivery with apprehension.

'I spoke to Jackson.'

Ayesha's hand flailed behind her, searching for a chair as her knees weakened.

'*Marshallah*! Goolam, I thought I knew her from somewhere and all the time you were telling me I was wrong,' she said in a voice that was barely above a whisper. 'What will we do now?'

Outside Elsie turned off the engine and sat hunched over the steering wheel. In her mind's eye she saw the woman's guileless dark eyes as she invited her back for a meal. Then she had a fleeting image of Rashid, the young boy, lying dead in the *veld*, a lock of hair fallen across his brow.

She had lied about her identity. Why? she wondered. Why hadn't she told them who she was? For a moment she was torn by indecision. Then quite abruptly she made up her mind. Since the trap was set for Wednesday, there would still be enough time to warn their son. Elsie climbed back out of the lorry watched by the surprised Jackson, and hurried back to the store.

THE NECKLACE

Early on Friday morning Burns Mpangela came into town in search of work, but wherever he went long queues of people were waiting. Here in the city he discovered the same sense of battered defeat that existed in the township. There was a feeling of hopelessness about waiting for a job when factories and businesses were closing their doors for good.

That day, however, Burns Mpangela was luckier than the rest. He found casual work at the marketplace. It was only a few hours' work and by noon when the job was over, Burns collected his pay and hurried off to the nearest bottle store where he spent all his earnings on a half-jack of brandy and a bottle of cheap *Lieberstein* wine.

Late that afternoon, struggling to get home in time for the curfew, he staggered towards the promenade. His throat worked convulsively, but the dry, foul taste of vomit remained in his mouth. He managed to get across the street, then stumbled, almost falling as the loose sole of his shoe caught on the concrete curb.

Once safely out of sight of the passers-by, his trembling hand reached into his pocket. The bottle was still there, nestling against his thigh, as warm and comforting as a woman's hand. For a moment his knees buckled and he leaned against the lamp standard for support, then he carefully eased the half-jack from his pocket.

Dismayed, Burns stared at the flat, empty bottle in his palm. With fluttering fingers he unscrewed the top and held the bottle to his lips. A single drop gathered near the neck, slowly rolling towards his impatient tongue where it disappeared with barely a trace. He drew his arm back, and tossed away the bottle. It arched through the air before hitting the sand with a muted plop.

The sky gathered the last remnants of light, and with the fast approaching darkness, Burns knew that he would not make it out of town in time for the curfew. A quick glance in either direction indicated that the coast was clear. He stumbled towards the low sandstone wall which ran along the promenade then clambered over, dropping heavily to the sand on the other side.

Two figures approached and he quickly backed into the shadows; a small wire-haired terrier bounding ahead, barked excitedly when it picked up his scent. Burns rolled into a ditch and waited for them to pass, but the terrier darted over to investigate and he gestured frantically to chase it away, fearful that its persistent yapping would draw attention to himself. Then at a whistle from its owner the dog dashed away.

Half-rising from the ditch after they had left, Burns peered over the edge. Apart from a few strollers, the beach was deserted. This was what life had come to, he mused. The Whites seldom ventured too far from home these days, exercising a form of self-imposed detention. For them the menacing darkness which lurked beyond their wrought-iron gates and along the fringes of their high-voltage security lights, held a new kind of terror.

In the receding light the tide had come in, spreading itself in spent bubbles against the sloping sand. Although he was a long way from home, he expected that as always he'd get there; if not that day then it would be the next.

The next morning Burns awakened with the sun beating down into the ditch. He crawled out, unsteadily making his way to the main street. It was early enough to escape detection and his presence elicited only casual glances from those Whites who strolled along the beachfront. They assumed that he was one of the garden boys who'd had a night out in the township.

By the time he reached the township the old thirst had returned. On his way home he stopped in at the *shebeen*, hoping that someone there would stand him a drink. Anything, even a can of Queenie's illicit gut-corroding beer, containing everything from piss to torch batteries, would have done the job.

Years ago he and Gentleman-Jim were capable of consuming billy-cans full of the concoction, usually ending up in the gutter vomiting their guts out, convinced that they were about to die.

When he got to the *shebeen* some of the Friday-night patrons were still drinking and the newcomers were in a generous mood, especially the fat man with the balding head. He was wearing a khaki dust-coat and Burns immediately recognised him as a driver.

'I was a driver too. Many years ago … about twelve years ago,' he told the man; 'I used to deliver new cars to Jo'burg when they came by ship from *iNigilani* and America.'

The man's surprised and disbelieving glance swept over Burns.

'Oh, yes,' Burns went on, drawing the back of his hand across his mouth. 'I used to drive for Ford.' His glance settled on the man's beer, making it clear that his story would require some inducement. The other man lost interest and Burns quickly threw in the bait. 'I tell you my friend, things were good in those times, until that one day.'

The man stared at the froth on his home-brewed beer, then turned his questioning glance on Burns.

Burns became animated. 'One day we were driving from Port Elizabeth. It was a rush delivery and it was hot like hell. Fifteen cars all in a convoy, all of us black drivers hot and tired. We stopped only to eat and piss in the bushes. Some of the fellows they had some half-jacks. Me, I never touched a drink when I was driving.'

The other man levelled a disbelieving glance at Burns.

Burns shook his head. 'Those days I never touched a drink while I was driving. You know what can happen. The policemen, they can stop you anytime for a search.'

83

'Uh hum,' the man agreed. The subject of police searches was one with which he was all too familiar. 'Those bastards wait along the side of the road to trap you.'

'*Ja*, don't I know that. Anyway, like I was saying, I was sober as a judge,' he laughed, his face collapsing into a drunken grimace. 'I was driving along Rissik, thinking about how much I'd earned on this trip ... when *boom!*' he crashed his fist into his open palm. 'Some white woman hit me in the rear-end at a light on Rissik Street. I thought the sky had fallen in. I was shaking like a leaf, and so was she until the police came. Damn woman told them that I had stopped at a green light. "Must be drunk," she said.'

The other man shook his head sympathetically and with his khaki handkerchief, wiped the perspiration from his bald head.

'All the witnesses came forward. Some white, some black. The Whites say I was in the wrong, the Blacks say she was in the wrong. In the end you know who they believed,' Burns said.

The man nodded. 'It always happens like that.'

'I was fired on the spot. The whole thing was written in my passbook that I was drunk and driving.' He sighed. 'I never got another job again.'

The fat man was moved by his misfortune and bought him a pail of Queenie's beer.

Burns nodded his head in appreciation. He paused, a far-away look in his eyes. 'My friend Gentleman-Jim used to say: "First they kill your spirit, then they kill your body".' He lapsed into thoughtful silence, his eyes moist. 'Gentleman-Jim was my friend. You know what happened to him?'

The man shook his head.

'They killed him three years ago, on his fiftieth birthday. The two of us was to meet, just down the road on Tenth Avenue. Right there by the river,' he said, pointing in that direction. 'We was to meet behind a clump of trees with a bottle, to shoot the breeze about the old days. Ten o' clock I was still waiting for the bastard. The bottle of wine in my

84

pocket.' He took a mouthful of beer, then sat there quietly grimacing at the pain brought on by these recollections. A white residue of malt formed around his mouth. 'I heard somebody coming. I thought it was Gentleman-Jim, but there were other voices ... strange voices. I ducked back behind the tree.'

The man, sensing that a drama was about to unfold, set his tin of *utywala* down on the ground before him. They were crouched in the backyard of the *shebeen*, away from the other customers.

'There they were,' Burns said, his voice dropping. 'Two of them carrying a torch of burning rags. Following behind them were some more people, shouting and laughing. I watched from behind the tree. Jesus!' The memory evoked a shudder. 'They were dragging him here, by the arms,' he said, indicating his arm-pits. 'The one with the torch, he ran back to help the others. Then I saw the face.' He paused sucking in his breath. 'It was Gentleman-Jim. Shoving him from behind with a stick was Weston Ndamase. Some people called him 'Stretch' because he was like a telephone pole. Skinny like a rat,' he said, showing his little finger. 'He was a policeman, and Gentleman-Jim had this big fight right here, in that doorway,' he said, turning to indicate the back door at Queenie's. 'Gentleman-Jim he called Weston a sell-out. Told him he'd sell his mother for a bottle of wine. I told him to shut up, but he wouldn't listen. I could see something terrible in Weston's face and I knew that someday he'd get even.' He lapsed into silence.

'What happened then?' the other man asked.

'My throat is a little dry from all this talking,' Burns replied.

The other man anxious to hear the conclusion, poured more than half his beer into Burns's tin.

'Thank you my friend,' Burns said and took a big gulp while his companion waited. 'I was shaking behind that tree. Then they poured something from a gallon can over a tyre. I smelt the petrol and I knew. Jesus, I knew.' He paused to take another mouthful of beer. 'They dropped the tyre around

85

Gentleman-Jim's neck. They call it "The Necklace", you know,' he explained, but the other man had heard many stories from the townships. 'Then they threw a match. I saw my friend's face.' Burns's voice broke and tears streamed down his face. He blew his nose into the sand and drew the sleeve of his grimy jacket across his face.

The other man dropped his glance. He had no doubt that the story was true. He finished his drink, made a few clucking noises to show his sympathy and then got to his feet.

'Don't go now, man. I'll tell you more about Gentleman-Jim.'

The other man drew up his shoulders. 'I got to go to work tonight.'

The man left and Burns remained on his haunches, his arms dangling at his sides, his head bowed over the empty tin of beer.

Gentleman-Jim had been his best friend. The only true friend he ever had. They had such good times together. Somehow in those early years it was easier to survive. But not so any more, he reflected, with a twinge of nostalgia for those bygone days.

He thought of the story his friend had taken such pleasure in telling; the one about the time he had come across a diamond on the banks of the Orange River, and how he had been cheated out of that same diamond by a fast-talking Scotsman. There were times when he wondered about the truth of this story, especially since each time it was told, the diamond increased in size. Had Gentleman-Jim lived long enough, Burns suspected, he might have needed a crane to have hauled this famous stone, if he had ever got it back from the Scotsman.

Burns sat there for hours, his head bowed, his thoughts fixed on the past, until Queenie lost patience with him around midnight and kicked him out. He spent the rest of Saturday night in the shell of a burnt-out car.

On Sunday morning he awakened with a start to a loud clamour. He shot bolt upright and glanced about nervously for the source of the commotion. In the distance youthful voices chanted above the drone of the lumbering dragons spewing death with such impunity.

Burns clasped his head and groaned. The noise grew louder. He wondered whether his fourteen-year-old daughter, Sophy, would be amidst the crowd. Scrambling out of the wreck, he hitched up his trousers and unsteadily made his way home. Ahead of him in a narrow street, children were scattered by exploding cannisters of tear gas. He flattened himself against a fence as they stampeded by. There was always danger even for bystanders; if not from the rioting youths, or the police in their tanks, then it came from the ubiquitous *tsotsis*.

He headed home along a rutted track euphemistically referred to as Second Avenue. The distant pop-pop of gunfire indicated that the police were again routing the children. He hastened along the lane of blackened palings towards Third Avenue; only a block from where the streets were barricaded. The pungent smell of burning rubber stung his eyes. A blast of hot wind climbed his trousers, overpowering him with the stench of urine and vomit.

If Sophy were home, he thought, Victoria wouldn't be quite so forbidding. But he knew this would not be likely, his daughter was seldom home these days. They were all too busy making a revolution, and burning their schools.

It frightened him that life wasn't simple any more. So many things terrified him these days. Alcohol was the only thing that helped to desensitise him. In a way it gave him the courage to face each new day, and it numbed him against the knowledge that one of these days they would be burying their daughter.

The parents all lived in fear of this. It was as inevitable as the rising sun, for a new tone of defiance had crept into these youthful confrontations. These children had no fear of death. Did they understand what it meant to die? Why did they disdain it? Was life really so unthinkable without a decent future? We lived with it, why couldn't they? he wondered.

What was happening to the children? What terrible anger had twisted them into such perversity?

'Sophy,' he muttered under his breath.

'You didn't do anything. You just let the white man shit on you!' She had screamed at him that time.

'What is the point of sacrificing your life?' her school principal had demanded during his eulogy at a student's funeral one day. 'Nothing will change. Your death like that of thousands of others, will only be another statistic in the newspapers littering the township.'

The man was right, Burns thought. What was the use of trying to get yourself killed? It was smarter to take it easy. Things were bound to get better. Couldn't she see that already Blacks were in jobs traditionally held by Whites, and some of them no less cocky than their white counterparts? Fighting would only make things worse; people would die and most of them would be black. The government said things would change. He had heard that the passbook was to be abolished. If this were so then it would wipe out his record and he would once again be eligible for a decent job. The thought pleased him no end, until he remembered that there were no jobs to be had.

He leaped over a pot-hole and teetered on the edge. His legs may have been unsteady, but his mind was crystal clear. 'They only know about making bombs, and about messing up a man's life,' he muttered crossly. 'No education. No jobs.'

'Without an education which of you will be able to run this country after you've done making your revolution?' he'd asked Sophy.

'We won't settle for their second-class education. We'll rather do without,' she had told him.

'An education is important. I never had one and look at me.' He paused, glancing away. 'You need an education to get a job. Without an education you're just a *dom kop*. I know you don't like what you're being taught in schools but education isn't only learning. It also has to do with how you use what you've learnt. You don't see the white man boycotting

88

schools, even though he's learning in Afrikaans too. His education goes on. He'll always be able to outwit you, because while you're out throwing stones he's studying. At this rate you'll never catch up with him.'

'It's either a decent education or nothing at all. And as for jobs ... You seem to forget that there are no jobs whether you have a certificate or not,' she snapped. 'The few jobs that are still available are being kept for the Whites. No, *Tata*, we'll make the sacrifices that you wouldn't make,' she had replied stubbornly. 'The rivers will run with blood. It will be our blood, but we will not give up until we win this war against our white oppressors.'

War. He didn't like that word. He sometimes worried that she was too old for her years. He tried to kick an empty can all the way across the street. It rolled a short distance and plopped into a pot-hole. Everywhere stinking pools of stagnant water had collected. There were no sewers and the dusty streets were dotted witn human and animal excrement.

Burns coughed, clearing his throat. What he needed was another drink for the courage to face Victoria, he thought as he wove his way down Second Avenue, shaking his head to dispel his morose thoughts before they took hold. He caught the smell of frying meat. Or was it the smell of burning flesh? These days it was hard to distinguish between the two. The thought turned his stomach and he doubled over to retch into the street.

After all the heaving was over, he straightened up, drew his sleeve across his mouth and continued his unsteady journey home. His next stop was at a smouldering rubbish heap. Still recognisable were the remains of a mattress and an old steel bedframe. A blackened shoe lay on the verge. He kicked it into the heap, the impact exposing a metal sign which advertised a product to prevent odour and decay.

He leaned over to see whether there was anything salvageable but the heat drove him back. Using a stick, he prodded the pile of ashes. 'Stop decay ... ', he read. It could only be a white man's sign because the Blacks lived with the effluvia of their rotting lives. It invaded their being and became part of their existence, hovering like the stench of death.

Suddenly he caught a sense of his own decay and his nostrils flared. He needed to relieve himself and reached into his open fly. He drew out his flaccid penis. Shit. It's dead, too, he groaned, watching the urine as it trickled against his trouser-leg. Then, tucking what remained of his masculinity into the gaping hole in his trousers, he staggered home.

When Aaron stopped his whimpering, Victoria knew that her husband was coming. '*Tata, Tata*,' the child cried. She caught Burns's scent and with sinking heart realised that he was drunk again.

Aaron, just four years old, turned his accusing glance on his mother. She had promised that his father would be bringing food, yet his hands were empty. '…*lambele*,' Aaron whimpered.

She knew then. 'Oh *Thixo*.'

Burns saw her expression and remembered that he had spent the money with which he was supposed to buy mealie-meal. The *tsotsis* got me,' he said leaning out of the window.

She looked up listlessly. She seemed very frail, almost ancient, her golden skin glistening. She remained motionless, her gaze oddly fixed, stark.

Her nose twitched, and she shook her head. 'The children are hungry. What are we going to do?' She turned her eyes in the direction of his voice. They were opaque and lifeless.

Burns was intimidated by the blank stare. She turned her sightless eyes from him. There were no tears. She had long since given up crying. What was the use? It never changed anything. You got up in the morning, struggled through the day, and then went to bed when the sun went down. If you were lucky, you made it through the night. The next day the same cycle started again. There were times when she thought her blindness was a blessing. She put her hands over her face in a gesture of weariness.

'Don't worry, tomorrow I'll find a job.'

She was silent, swaying from side to side with her hands over her face.

'I'll try in town again,' he assured her.

She removed her hands. 'Where? Where will you find a job? There's no work for anyone. The factories are closing. All those people out there are looking for jobs, too.' She gestured expansively and turned her head from him. 'Where will we go when they burn down this shack?' she asked.

He staggered forward. She did not flinch, merely sat there with a dignity so imposing that in a flash of drunken imagery, he saw before him a Xhosa princess, resplendent on her throne. He blinked to clear his vision. It was only his wife, Victoria, blinded by a disease which had followed the birth of Sophy. She sat on the bare floor of the shanty, head crowned by her turban, the old blouse ripped, one breast exposed.

'All I want,' Victoria had said one evening, her sightless eyes turned towards the Heavens, 'is for you to find a decent job so that we can feed the children. It would have been good for Sophy to become a teacher, but now all I want is for her to stay out of trouble.' Then after a long thoughtful pause, she added, 'Perhaps someday when you get a job I'd like to have a bed; a wooden bed with a mattress, and maybe a table, and some plates.' This was the extent of her dream.

Burns liked to dream, too. In the early days when Gentleman-Jim was alive, they used to philosophise about life. Now as he looked back on all of this, it seemed that the same questions always surfaced: Were they not people, too? Did they not want the same thing as the Whites who had homes, jobs and food, and who could live and work wherever they chose? 'Why are we different?' he had asked Gentleman-Jim. 'Do we not bleed, die, kiss, cherish or make babies in the same way? Do we not have two arms and two legs; faces, eyes and hearts which beat to the same rhythm?'

'You're a fucking man. Don't you worry about what the white man says or thinks about you. The only way they can change what you are is by cutting off what you have,' Gentleman-Jim had told him once.

Aaron started whimpering again. 'The child is hungry,' Victoria said. She drew the boy against her, furious with Burns and his lack of responsibility.

Aaron's whimpers turned into a loud wail.

'Shut him up,' Burns snapped impatiently, but his anger was self-directed.

'No, let him cry! At least it tells me that he is still alive.'

'I'll find something to eat. I'll borrow some mealie-meal from Ousisie.'

She shrugged. 'You stink.' He stepped away from her, and his quick movement stirred the air, sending up draughts of the stench.

There were no household taps or bathrooms. The communal taps were a few blocks away beside the lavatories which consisted of crude sanitation pits filled with rubbish dumped there by the rebellious children. To do their business people went into the *veld*, or squatted behind their shanties. On hot days the stench and flies were unbearable.

His wife, sensing his hesitation, wordlessly handed him a sliver of Lifebuoy soap.

The pop of machine-gun fire reached them. The armoured vehicles were again patrolling the periphery.

'They'll all be killed. Have you seen Sophy?' she cried as the sounds grew louder.

He shook his head.

'You'd better call her. They'll kill her.'

Aaron started whimpering again.

'*Tsak*,' she whispered, making a sound with her teeth. Her breast hung from her open blouse, like an empty sock, the veins distended and throbbing. Although her milk had dried up a long time ago she suckled Aaron hoping to keep him quiet. She sat impassively with her back against the board which formed the one wall of their shack, grimacing in pain as the boy's teeth clenched around her nipple.

Burns squared his jaw and hurried away. At the corner he

turned to glance back. She was still sitting exactly as he had left her. How could he fight what was happening to them? He had been stripped of everything, including his manhood. Like a pot simmering over a slow fire, he felt a stirring of emotion. An anger was slowly bubbling to the surface. 'Fucking bastards!' he shouted, kicking a dried mealie cob which soared into the air like a torpedo.

He hurried towards the river, the torn sole of his one shoe flapping against his bare foot. The rage grew until he thought that he would choke on it. He reached the river and leaped in fully clothed, dunking his head under, and staying down until his lungs felt as if they would burst. He surfaced, taking great gulps of air.

Burns thrashed the water, impressions of Gentleman-Jim, the 'Necklace', Sophy, and the horror that was the township collided like half-realised images from a nightmare. He dragged his clothes off, tossing them aside. His jacket ballooned, floated, and then sank to the bottom.

Burns drew himself erect, his bare feet digging into the sand at the bottom of the river. Then gripped by an uncontrollable urge, he clenched his fist and threw his head back, howling like a wounded jackal. For that moment he felt a surge of strength. It seemed to course through his veins like bolts of electricity.

Then his vision cleared, the red haze lifted and he saw once again the palls of smoke rising from the burning barricades.

CARDBOARD MANSIONS

'Chotoo! Eh Chotoo!'

'*Ja*, Dadi-Ma?' the boy cried from the far side of the yard.

'Don't *ja* Dadi-Ma, me! Come here!' the old woman called from the *stoep*. Leaning over the low abutment wall, she craned to peer around the corner but her view was obstructed by a pile of rubbish. She stepped back knocking over the chipped enamel pail which was normally kept beside her bed at night. The empty pail rolled out of reach, clattering against the wall.

She waited for the boy, pulling the end of the faded green cotton sari over her head. Her wide, flat heels hung over the back of the blue rubber thongs almost two sizes smaller than her feet.

Dadi-Ma looked much older than her seventy-three years. She was a tall, heavily-built woman with slow, tired movements. Her dark brown eyes were set deep in a face scored and marked with age and hardship. The gap in the front of her mouth was relieved only by three stumps of rotted teeth, bloodily stained by betel-nut.

In her youth she had been much admired for her beauty, with her dark lustrous eyes like those of a young doe. But there was no one left to remember her as she'd been then. Sonny, the youngest of her sons, and her grandson, Chotoo, were the only surviving members of her family. Three of her sons and her husband, like so many of the men who had toiled in the sugar-cane fields, had all died of tuberculosis.

And now the only ones left to her were her grandchild, Chotoo, and her friend Ratnadevi. Dadi-Ma in her old age was left to gaze upon the world with the patient endurance of the old water buffalo they had once owned in India.

94

The boy, Chotoo, took a long time coming. His grand-mother waited, her broad, varicose-veined feet and legs planted astride. A rip in her sari revealed a discoloured slip, unadorned and frayed. Her dark eyes stared out from under thick brows, slowly gathering in impatience.

'Chotoo!' she called again and sat down on the step to wait.

The row of shanties were all connected. At one time they had served as a shed, but an enterprising landlord had used sheets of corrugated iron to divide the shed into stalls which he rented to the poor. All the dividing walls stopped at least twelve inches short of the ceiling.

On Saturday nights when Frank Chetty beat his wife, Nirmala, her cries swirled over the heads of the other tenants. Some ignored them. Others were just grateful that they were not in Nirmala's shoes. Dadi-Ma's daughter-in-law, Neela, had once remarked to their neighbour, Urmila, that no matter what Sonny was guilty of, this was one thing that he had not yet stooped to.

'Just you wait and see,' Urmila said. 'It'll happen when Sonny loses his job.'

But even when Sonny lost his job he never raised a hand to his wife. Chotoo, however, was not so lucky and in his short life had been slapped many times, often for no apparent reason. Despite this, Dadi-Ma's pride in her son remained undiminished. She could hold up her head and say that he had never lifted a hand to his wife or his mother.

It had come as a terrible blow to Dadi-Ma when Neela had died in childbirth three years ago, leaving Sonny with the boy, Chotoo. But Sonny was hardly ever around and everything had fallen on her shoulders. Somehow they managed. Even when Sonny lost his job they still managed. Dadi-Ma used many of the ideas she had picked up from Ratnadevi who had a real knack for making do.

But eventually Sonny had fallen in with a bad crowd and everything seemed to come apart. Now there was a new element in their struggle; one that caused Dadi-Ma a great deal of anxiety. As Sonny was jobless, there was not a penny coming in any more, yet all weekend long Sonny smoked *dagga*. Sometimes he drew the reefers through a broken bottle-neck making himself so crazy that he'd end up running amok with a knife. At times like these Dadi-Ma and Chotoo had to hide from him until the effects of the *dagga* wore off.

Without means to pay the rent there was constant friction between himself and the landlord. Sonny, desperate and irritable, pleaded with the landlord until they reached a state of open hostility. The tenants were all drawn into this conflict, all except Dadi-Ma. She alone remained aloof and detached. Sitting on the concrete step in front of their room, she listened in silence to the two men arguing when the landlord came to collect the rent. Sonny's response was always wild and abusive. Although she was afraid that he would harm the landlord, she remained impassive.

The landlord, Mr Naidoo, grew to resent the old woman. He thought that her silence was a way of showing contempt for him. Who was she to judge him, a man of means and property? He often wondered as he drove off in his Mercedes why it was that she never said anything. What thoughts crossed her mind as she sat there implacable as a stone Buddha? In the end he grew to hate the old woman.

Then one day the inevitable happened: Sonny got into a drunken brawl and stabbed someone. He was arrested, sentenced and thrown into jail. Mr Naidoo saw his opportunity to evict the old woman, but he hesitated fearing censure from the other tenants, some of whom had contributed to help Dadi-Ma with her rent. He knew, though, that this situation could not continue indefinitely. Those who had supported her were themselves experiencing difficulty. So he bided his time.

It happened that a few months later the old woman fell so far behind with her rent that the others could no longer assist her. Now at last Mr Naidoo could exercise his rights; he gave Dadi-Ma her notice.

She was devastated. She had tried so hard to keep the roof over their heads. There was nothing for her to do now but pack their few possessions. They would have to move, but where to? she fretted. Dadi-Ma's concern was more for her grandson than for herself. She did not have many more years left, but what would happen to this boy who was only starting out in life?

'What took you so long, hey?' Dadi-Ma demanded, feigning severity when the boy finally joined her.

He shrugged, his hands thrust deep in his pockets, emulating the cockiness of the older boys who hung out in the alley. She tousled his hair and he sat down on the step beside her, pressing close to her side where he felt safe and secure.

For a time they sat like this in silence, the boy content with this closeness while his grandmother brooded about the past and the problems which were driving them into the unknown. Her mind moved slowly and ponderously, like an ox picking its way over the stones, lingering on the good times.

Lately her thoughts had started returning to those happy years; to Ratnadevi and Stanger. The two women had shared a friendship that went back a long way. They had arrived on the same boat from India to marry two indentured labourers on the sugar-cane fields in Natal. They had lived in the same compound, as close as sisters, sharing in each other's joys and tragedies.

'Why you like the *skollies*?' the old woman asked the boy, adjusting the sari over her head. 'They no good.'

'Why you say that Dadi-Ma?' he asked. His enormous brown eyes turned up to her questioningly.

He was so young, she thought, how could he understand that she wanted him to make something of his life? How could he understand that if he didn't try, this was all he had to look forward to?

'Because they bad. They smoke *dagga*. You best go to school so you can be something hey?' she said in her broken English.

'We don't do nothing wrong Dadi-Ma, we just sit out there bullshitting.'

The old woman shook her head wearily.

97

'They say old man Naidoo going to throw us out. Where we going to go Dadi-Ma?'

Dadi-Ma felt a deep attachment to her grandson. She had been drawn to him from the moment he was born. It had been Dadi-Ma who took care of him right from that first day, not his mother who was too tired and sickly to care. From Chotoo, came the only warmth and caring that life still apportioned to her. All that the boy had known of love and tenderness came from her; not from his mother, whom he could not remember. It was a bond that neither had words for. The only expression Dadi-Ma ever gave her grandson of her feelings, was a rare and awkward pat on his cheek, or the tousling of his hair with her arthritic fingers.

The boy, undernourished and small for his age, with eyes as large and expressive as hers had once been, was conscious of his grandmother's love. The others, like his parents, had deserted him. But not her. She was the fulcrum in his fragile existence.

'I was thinking Chotoo, maybe you and me, we go to Stanger. It will be a good place for us. This place is no good,' she muttered.

'Where is Stanger, Dadi-Ma?' he asked, his voice catching in breathless excitement.

'It's not so far away.'

'How will we go ... by car, by train?' he asked, in his shrill little voice.

She nodded, smiling down at him. 'We go by train.'

Dadi-Ma had saved some money for just such an emergency. The money, fifty rands, was what she had amassed in her long lifetime. Money that she had artfully secreted. Many times the money had gone for some other emergency but somehow she had always managed to replace it. Sometimes it had been slow to accumulate; money from the sale of a few pieces of gold jewellery brought with her from India, a few cents here and there from what she could scrimp out of the money Sonny had given her to buy food and clothes in the good old days when he still had a job.

98

These savings were all that stood between them and destitution now. The previous night she had removed the money from its hiding place beneath the linoleum under her bed, and in the dim light of the lamp she had counted it carefully, stacking the small coins in even piles, smoothing out the crumpled notes. Then she had returned it to the hiding place for safe keeping.

After a while Chotoo started fidgeting and wriggled out from under her arm.

'You don't tell nobody,' Dadi-Ma warned him. 'If old man Naidoo find out he make big trouble for us.'

Chotoo nodded. Despite his age, he understood. 'Can I go and play now, Dadi-Ma?'

'*Ja*, you go and play, but you remember what I tell you.'

'I won't tell nobody, Dadi-Ma.'

She nodded and he sauntered off to the side of the house where the *dagga* smokers hung out. She watched him go, legs thin and scaly, the knobbly knees protruding just below his short trousers, his feet rough and thickened from going barefoot.

The tenement somehow always reminded Dadi-Ma of the quarters they had once occupied on the sugar-cane plantation. There she and her husband had lived in a barracks with dozens of other workers, separated from the rest by paper-thin walls, or frayed curtains. In summer the windowless barracks were like ovens and then when the rains came it was like the monsoons in India, lasting for weeks and turning the compound into a quagmire.

Further north along the east coast, was the town of Stanger where Ratnadevi had eventually moved after her husband died. His death had released Ratnadevi and her family from the contract which had bound them to the plantation. When Dadi-Ma's own husband had died and Sonny had run off to the city, Dadi-Ma had also moved to Stanger to live with Ratnadevi.

She remembered every detail so clearly. The wooden shack set back from the road amidst a clump of mango, banana and

99

litchi trees. There had been an abundance of everything on that small piece of property, even the birds flocked to feed off the ripening fruit. It was indeed a wonderful sight and one that Dadi-Ma had cherished since that time.

She had never been happier than during those days with Ratnadevi in that old shack in Stanger. The two of them had managed by taking in laundry from the white people, most of whom were English-speaking. They also used to weave baskets which they sold in the local community, or peddled in the market place where Ratnadevi had a hawker's barrow.

The house was at the end of a gravel road. It was the last house on the street with a large corner lot where parts of an old picket-fence still stood. On windy nights they could hear the pickets clattering and rattling against each other. Each sound had its own particular significance and was like music to Dadi-Ma's ears. Some nights when it was very quiet she imagined she could hear the strains of a flute, the same poignant sounds made by Manu, the confectioner in her village in India, when he sat on the front step of his hut playing to the night.

From one of the big trees in the front-yard hung a swing carved from an old tyre. There had been enough room for a large garden and the eggs produced by the hens were taken to the market each day. Dadi-Ma learnt a great deal about survival from the years she had spent there.

Then to interrupt this happiness, something unexpected had happened which irreversibly altered the tempo of her life. Sonny, who had married and moved to Port Elizabeth, sent for her. He was her son; her only son, how could she have refused him? Without the slightest hesitation, Dadi-Ma packed her few belongings and went to live with her son and Neela, her daughter-in-law. Neela, she found, was a frail and sickly girl who was unable to withstand the rigours of married life. Dadi-Ma took care of them all.

Several years went by and to Dadi-Ma's dismay her daughter-in-law, Neela, had still not produced a child. For reasons that Dadi-Ma did not understand the young girl could not carry a single pregnancy to its full term, miscarrying each after only four months.

It was a difficult life but Dadi-Ma never complained, even though she hated city life, and constantly longed for Stanger and for Ratnadevi. The years passed and memories of those happy years began to dim. Eventually she stopped thinking about them. For fifteen years she lived with Sonny and his wife, taking care of them, and suffering constant abuse at the hands of Neela who grew resentful of her role in the house. Then one day, five years ago, Neela gave birth to Chotoo and it was as though Dadi-Ma had finally found fulfilment.

Now, ever since the landlord had given them notice, her thoughts returned again to that little house at the end of the road with the swing in the front-yard. She could see the trees and hear the plank verandah and fence creaking in the wind.

Dadi-Ma remained on the step, dreaming. There was a stench of urine and human excrement in the air which came from a blocked sewer. They were accustomed to the stench which mingled with the rancid smell of old *ghee* and curry.

In a way Dadi-Ma was relieved that they were leaving. It was too difficult to raise a boy in this environment. He needed to run free, to breathe air unpolluted by smoke and odours of decay. Dadi-Ma's thoughts drifted back to the long low line of hills in the north, to mango and litchi trees laden with fruit. She remembered how she and Ratnadevi had sat out on the verandah, identifying the gaily coloured birds as they swooped down into the trees.

She and Ratnadevi had spent so much of their time in the backyard, doing the wash, kneading and scrubbing the heavy linen against the fluted surface of the washboard. In their spare time they sat beneath the tree, weaving baskets. Sometimes they chatted about their life in India, or life on the plantation; other times they worked in easy companionable silence.

Chotoo returned to his grandmother's side, wanting to know more about this place called Stanger. She was smiling to herself now as she thought of how she and Ratnadevi would once again sit out in the yard. She remembered the long washing line and the sputtering sizzle as Ratnadevi deftly spat against the iron. She remembered the smell of lye and freshly ironed laundry.

They could weave baskets again. As if following her thoughts, her fingers now stiff with age and arthritis, fell awkwardly into the familiar movements of weaving. The boy seeing this, pressed closer to her side. She looked down upon him sombrely and drew his head against her chest. She began to talk to him of the life she had once known. The boy listened and with her words felt a new sense of adventure.

That night Dadi-Ma bundled together their few possessions. Her plan was to leave under cover of darkness since she did not have the money to pay the landlord the rent that was owing.

They caught the train for Durban early the next morning. For Chotoo the adventure had begun. Through most of the journey he was awake, his nose flattened against the window. In the second-class coach, they shared their compartment with two other women, who chatted amiably with his grandmother while he remained at her side.

When they arrived in Durban, he grabbed a handful of his grandmother's sari, and hung on while she carried the bundle of belongings on her head. In the street outside the station they got into the bus for Stanger.

It was a long drive and they passed fields of sugar-cane. Dadi-Ma pointed out many things to him, drawing his attention to this or to that. He stood against the seat, his nose once again pressed to the window, lurching against her as the bus bumped and swayed. They stopped often to offload passengers on the road and it was afternoon before they arrived at their destination.

Dadi-Ma became excited as they approached the town. She asked the woman across the aisle about the bus stop. The woman told her that the bus went all the way to the market. Dadi-Ma was pleased. She knew her way from there.

They entered the town and Dadi-Ma looked around for familiar landmarks, but things had changed. The market was no longer where she had remembered it to be. It had been moved to a new location. Dadi-Ma was puzzled. She spoke to the woman again, asking where the old market was, but the woman shrugged, saying she didn't know. She did not live here, only visited occasionally.

'Ask the woman over there,' she said.

Dadi-Ma got up from her seat and Chotoo followed her, clutching the end of her sari. In her anxiety she was impatient with him. 'Stay there,' she snapped.

Chotoo's eyes grew large and mournful and she was sorry that she had spoken sharply. She touched his cheek and explained that she would be back in a moment, that she was merely going to speak to the woman over there, near the front of the bus. She told him to remain in the seat so that no one could take it.

Chotoo understood and hung back.

Dadi-Ma spoke to this other woman for several minutes. Chotoo watched her and sensed her unease.

'What is it Dadi-Ma?' he asked when she returned.

'We will have to walk a long distance,' she told him.

'Why?' he asked.

'So many questions!' she exclaimed. Then she said, 'The market-place where the bus stops, is no longer where I thought it would be, they have moved it.'

The boy did not say anything; he sensed in her a new anxiety that bewildered him.

When they got off the bus at the market-place, the woman Dadi-Ma had talked to in the front of the bus, asked why they wanted to get to that particular street.

'It is where my friend Ratnadevi lives,' she said.

'Your friend lives there?' the woman asked, surprised.

'Yes, she has a small house with big trees.'

The woman fell silent. Then she shrugged her shoulders. Perhaps this friend was a servant in one of the big houses out there, she concluded.

Dadi-Ma smiled and thanked the woman.

The woman repeated her instructions telling them to go to the end of the wide road and then to turn to the left and continue on for five more streets to where there was a big store. At that point they were to turn right and walk for several blocks until they reached the area of big houses and mansions. There they were to turn right again to the street Dadi-Ma was enquiring about. 'But there is no small house there like the one you have described,' the woman said.

'From there I will know my way,' Dadi-Ma assured her. She thanked the woman, hoisted the bundle onto her head, and waited for Chotoo to get a good grip on her sari. Then she left. Her feet in the old *champals* flip-flopped as she walked away. The other woman watched them going.

Dadi-Ma and Chotoo walked a long way that day, stopping often to rest. Chotoo was tired and dragged on her sari and she had to urge him on with quiet words of encouragement. She talked about the trees and the birds, nurturing the anticipation which lightened his step. At the end of the road, they stopped. She took down the bundle from her head and carefully unwrapped it. Packed amongst their belongings was a bottle of water. She handed it to Chotoo who took a long drink, then after taking a sip herself, she screwed the cap back on and returned the bundle to her head.

They turned left and continued on. She recognised some of the landmarks, her heart lurching excitedly as she pointed these out to the boy. Then they turned right and suddenly nothing seemed familiar any more.

Nevertheless they pressed on, following the woman's directions. They walked all the way to the end of the street in silence. On both sides of the street were large houses surrounded by walls and fences. The open field she remembered was no longer there. Her legs automatically propelled her forward. The pain that had racked her limbs through the past few days now gave way to fear which turned her legs to jelly.

They had made the last right turn and supposedly this was the street where she had once lived. Her dark eyes looked out upon an area that was unrecognisable. Slowly and wearily they made their way to the end of the street, but Ratnadevi's house was no longer there, neither were the trees and the groves of bamboo. She took the bundle from her head. The boy raised his eyes to look at her. In her face he saw the bewilderment.

Dadi-Ma was tired now, her legs could no longer hold her weight and she sat down on the curb, drawing the boy down beside her.

'What's wrong Dadi-Ma? Where is Ratnadevi's house?'

Dadi-Ma's fingers moved, weaving an invisible basket.

'Dadi-Ma?' he said in a small voice.

'Hush Chotoo. Don't worry. We'll rest a bit and then we'll find Ratnadevi's house.'

Chotoo drew close to his grandmother, resting his head on her lap for he was tired and sleepy.

The woman must have made a mistake, she thought. Ratnadevi's house was probably at the end of some other street and she would find it. A small house with a plank verandah and many trees with birds. Chotoo would be able to climb trees and pick fruit to his heart's content and sometimes he'd help them to pick bamboo for baskets.

A servant who had seen them sitting there, came out of one of the houses. 'Why are you sitting here?' she asked.

Dadi-Ma described the house she was searching for.

'Yes, I remember that one,' the woman said. 'The house was torn down a long time ago.'

'What happened to the people who once lived here?' Dadi-Ma asked.

The woman shrugged and shook her head.

Dadi-Ma sat back, the pain that had nagged her all day numbing her arms, suddenly swelled in her chest. The woman noticed the way Dadi-Ma's colour had changed.

'Are you all right, Auntie?' she asked.

Dadi-Ma compressed her lips and nodded. She did not want to alarm Chotoo. Did not want him to be afraid. She struggled to get up, the woman helping her to her feet.

But Chotoo saw the expression on his grandmother's face and for the first time in his life he felt insecure and uncertain about the future; felt a dreadful apprehension of being wrenched from the only human being he had ever loved.

'Dadi-Ma, Dadi-Ma,' he sobbed.

'It's all right Chotoo, it's all right.'

But he knew that it wasn't all right, that it would never be all right again.

NTOMBI

In the distance something approached. It was still no more than a speck on the horizon of this vast, flat and desolate plain. A young boy waited, tense and anxious, his hands clenched around his *knobkierie*. He peered into the distance fearing that it might be the jackal.

The flock of sheep entrusted to his care milled about at the foot of the *kopje*. Scrambling down the hillock to where they were grazing, he moved them to the far side. Then mindful of his own safety, he clambered out of harm's way to the top of a large rock.

The speck grew larger and finally, with intense relief, he was able to identify the approaching figure as that of a woman, not a jackal. He watched her come closer and he could tell by the way her stride faltered that she was exhausted.

Rising majestically from the palm of the *karoo* were two conical hills. When Ntombi saw this formation she knew that she had almost reached her destination. The last of her water had all been used up in her trek through the desolate *veld*. In the scorching sun her thirst had become unbearable. But now with the *kopjes* in sight she felt a new surge of strength. Throwing her shoulders back she raised her head, carrying herself with the pride and dignity befitting the daughter of Chief England Makalima.

Around her shoulders she wore an ecru blanket which protected the infant strapped to her back. With each step the frayed edges of the blanket slapped against her voluminous skirt. Wrapped in superb folds around her head was an enormous black turban reminiscent of Arab head-dresses.

The twin hillocks loomed up ahead and not another creature stirred under the sun which poured its heat over the flaccid, dust-covered leaves of the bushes; each clump, a family of plants, huddled together for mutual support. Here in this infinite space, encapsulated in a sense of timelessness with only the breeze interrupting the silence, she hoped to make a new home for herself and the child she had conceived by the white man, Conrad Schoeman.

The name, Ntombi, a corruption of *intombi*, was an Xhosa word for 'little girl'. It was the pet-name her father had once used before he had turned away from her disappointed and bitter.

She and Schoeman had met by the Doring River which flowed through a wide gully about a mile from the mission school. A shallow, muddy creek for most of the year, it ran clear and deep for two months following the spring rains.

One Friday afternoon, school was dismissed early and the students stayed to help Father Mkantini clear a stretch of *veld* to be used as a soccer field. Since there was nothing she could help with, she decided that she would do her washing by the river. She was the only one there that afternoon. The other women from the village had already been and gone, and as she knelt in the sand, pounding her clothes on the rocks, she missed their gossip and silly laughter. When her washing was done and she had spread her wet blanket on the ground, she stripped down to her cotton petticoat and waded into the water, unaware that she was being observed from the top of the embankment.

Conrad Schoeman sat astride his horse and watched her through his binoculars. She stepped out of the water and the wet fabric of her petticoat clung seductively to her body.

Ntombi, still oblivious to the presence of the stranger, searched for a stone to use on her roughened heels. She leaned over to scrub her feet while the sun shone through her undergarment, outlining her dark form; the shape so firm and rounded that it seemed as if it had been carved from a chunk of mahogany.

Conrad returned his glasses to their case, and negotiated his horse across the rocks to the narrow strip of beach where Ntombi was preoccupied with her toilet. He came up so silently that she heard him only when he was almost upon her. She swung around, dark eyes widening in startled surprise.

'*Molo*,' he greeted.

But Ntombi was too shaken to respond.

'I'm sorry I frightened you. I saw you from a distance and I thought you would hear me coming.'

Ntombi, conscious of his glance and her partial state of undress, inched over to where her blanket was drying.

The horse, impatient to get to the water, pawed the ground and sent a shower of gravel into the air. Conrad Schoeman tightened his grip on the reins while Ntombi increased her distance from him.

He lifted his hat and a skirt of silver hair glinted in the sun. Raising his arm against his forehead he dabbed at the sweat on his brow. 'The sun is hot,' he remarked.

She nodded and removed her glance to a point in the distance. 'Yes,' she agreed, 'the sun is hot.'

He dismounted and led his horse to the water and she took this opportunity to tie the blanket about herself.

'You're not from these parts,' she said, watching him with curiosity.

He did not answer, but drank thirstily, splashing his face, and shaking his head. Drops of water sprayed in all directions like a wet dog shaking itself. Then he smoothed down his damp hair, replaced his hat and drew the back of his hand across his lips. He patted the horse and nudged it away from the water's edge.

'I come from the *karoo*,' he replied. 'What about you? Where have you come from?'

'My village is on the far side of the mountain.' She pointed north. 'But those of us who teach at the mission live near the school.'

'Where is the school?' he asked.

109

'You cannot see it from here. It is a mile beyond the trees. Past the place where one rock is balanced on another.'

Through his binoculars he had seen the gigantic sandstone rock balanced on a smaller one, the larger rock hanging so delicately that it seemed the slightest touch would send it crashing over.

'I have to go now,' Ntombi said shyly, gathering her damp laundry and carefully packing it into the four-gallon paraffin tin that had been cut in half.

Fascinated, Conrad Schoeman watched her lifting the tin of laundry onto her head, detecting a quality of hauteur in the tilt of her head and the way her feet were planted apart. A sudden poignant sadness clouded her eyes before she lowered her lids. She had remembered in that moment that *her* life was hedged by laws and restrictions.

He accompanied her to the mission, walking beside her along the rutted footpath.

Here, miles from civilisation, they were just man and woman; colour and class were of no consequence.

Trudging through the *veld*, Ntombi put her arms behind her and patted her son affectionately. In the pocket of her skirt was Conrad's gold watch and chain. He had given it to her on the day he left. 'Keep it for me,' he had told her. 'It has great meaning. It once belonged to my father. Someday I'll return for it.'

'She has let a white man buy her off with shiny trinkets, just like his ancestors did when they stole our land with beads and mirrors,' her father had told her mother, his lips curling contemptuously. 'Does she think that the white man will give up his wife for her? She says he will return for this trifle,' he had said, disdainfully dangling the watch from its chain. 'I say she will never set eyes on him again.'

When Ntombi's condition became obvious, she had tendered her resignation. She was a good teacher and Father Mkantini was sorry to see her go. He suggested that she should return following the birth of the baby, but Ntombi had

110

other plans.

Ntombi had spent much of her time by the river while she waited for the arrival of her baby. She hoped that with the strength of her love she could draw Conrad Schoeman back to that same spot. But the days passed and he did not return. She realised that she would have to go to him. While silently enduring her father's derision, Ntombi planned her journey to Diepkloof.

It had taken her two days to get to the twin *kopjes* which were Diepkloof landmarks. During the long nights of waiting, she had recalled every detail of the stories he had told her about his life here, and though she was seeing everything for the first time there was a feeling that she'd been there before. The journey had been much more difficult than she had anticipated, especially with a baby on her back. It was only her stubborn pride that carried her along. Now she was almost there. She shook her head freeing herself of her past, and the shimmering images of lakes and trees which, like a siren's song, had tried to lure her away from her course, abruptly disappeared. She calculated that Diepkloof, could not be much further. The twin mounds were just ahead. At that moment she didn't dare to think about her thirst, her dry throat or her swollen lips.

The young boy scrambled halfway down and hid behind a large boulder. Overcome by weariness Ntombi sank to the ground in the shade of an ironstone ledge. The air shimmered and danced in the heat, even the lizards darted away to find shelter beneath the rocks. With unsteady hands she undid the blanket, then carefully slid her son around to the front, hugging him against her chest, his head nestling between her breasts.

Ntombi's dark eyes traced the contours of his face, so much like his father's. An unexpected sound behind her abruptly ended her reflections. The head with its dramatic head-dress came up. She swung around, and her startled glance met the curious eyes of the young boy. For the first time now she noticed the small flock of sheep grazing on clumps of

111

vegetation at the foot of the *kopje*.

'*Molo, buti*,' she greeted, addressing him in the familiar form of the dialect.

'*Molo*,' he replied.

Ntombi smiled, her lips trembling with pain and discomfort. 'Do you know where I can find water?'

He nodded shyly, before scrambling down to where the sheep grazed. When he reached the foot of the *kopje* he leaped to his feet, almost losing his oversized trousers in the process, and pointed to a clump of plants. She understood and followed him down, carefully carrying her baby against her hip. Amidst the *karoo* bushes was a small plant with tiny beads of moisture covering its fleshy leaves. She twisted the plant off at its root and returned to the shelter beneath the ledge. She sat down again and solemnly thanked him, but he remained aloof, only his eyes darting as they followed her movements.

In spite of the heat the boy was wearing an enormous jacket. The rolled-up sleeves revealed wrists so slight that she could easily have circled them with thumb and forefinger. He leaned on his *knobkierie*, one foot hooked behind his leg, a bony knee protruding through the frayed tear in his trousers.

'Your *kierie* is a big one for a small person such as yourself.' Ntombi watched him, eyes glinting with amusement. She sucked the moisture from the plant, then removed the membrane and dabbed the fleshy leaf against her lips. At first it stung the dry, cracked surface of her skin, but she soon experienced its soothing effects.

Ntombi was accustomed to being with young children from her teaching days at the mission school. She was quite at ease with the young boy and even managed to coax a smile out of him. He almost laughed out aloud when she told him that her lips felt like *leguan* skin, but he was still cautious about being with a stranger and shyly covered his mouth with one hand while lowering his head.

'Are you from this farm … Diepkloof?'

He nodded.

'What is your name?'

112

'Tollie,' he said.

The baby thrashed impatiently and she freed her breast. With a sigh the little mouth closed around her nipple, anxious hands kneading her engorged breast. The sound of its greedy suckling intensified in the immense silence of the *veld*.

'How long have you been here?' she asked the boy.

'A long time.'

'Where do you live?' She waited patiently for his answer while she picked bits of fluff from the child's hair, so much lighter than her own.

The boy spoke Xhosa, but she noticed that he was small with the long neck and round head which was a physical trait of the Bushmen.

'Where is the house of this farm?' she enquired in Xhosa.

He turned slowly, pivoting on one foot like a dancer, and glanced in that direction.

She followed his gaze. In the distance she saw the outline of the big, white house.

While the baby fed, she talked to the boy about many things, but never once did she enquire about Conrad Schoeman, although she was tempted to. After the baby had had its fill, she covered her breast and set the child down on the ground. 'Will you watch him, *buti*, while I go to the top to see?' she asked.

'I have to watch my sheep,' Tollie protested, but did not move from where he stood.

'Your sheep will come to no harm here,' she told him.

'There is a big jackal ... '

'Tsak.' She clicked her tongue impatiently. 'All the more reason why you should watch the child, *kaloko*, the child is more important than the sheep,' she said, and proceeded to make her way over the smooth ironstone rocks, some of them in such regular layers, it seemed quite conceivable that they might have been put there by a stone-mason.

Tollie rose on his toes to take another look at the child, then his glance wandered to its mother who was clambering to the top of the *kopje* on all fours.

113

Ntombi reached the summit. The top was flat, like an inverted cone with the point sliced off. She dragged herself onto the top and stood upright, Conrad's watch weighting her pocket. She placed her hands on her hips, arched her back to relieve the tension, and surveyed the surrounding *veld*. In the still, clear air she could see the rocks on a hill miles away as if they were there beside her. A slight breeze kissed her cheek and then died away. The stillness that followed was so intense that she could hear the pounding of her heart.

Ntombi lifted her glance. She had no doubt that the big house would be just as Conrad had described it. She took a deep breath, as though to fortify herself against an ordeal that was yet to come.

Lost in thoughts about her baby and the anticipation of being reunited with Conrad, she forgot that she was standing on the summit of the *kopje*. She turned excitedly, missed her footing, and for a brief instant teetered on the edge, arms flailing wildly.

Tollie looked up when he heard her cry. Transfixed in horror he watched her plummet through the air. Her head struck the ledge and with a soft, sickening thud her body hit the ground. The figure was deathly still, the blood darkly crimson against her brown skin. He saw something glistening in the sand beside her and picked up the gold watch.

He was too shocked by events to stop and examine what he was holding. He gazed around frantically, seeking help, but he was all alone in the *veld*, surrounded only by his sheep. In a wild panic he plunged through the grazing flock, scattering them. Awakened by the noise the baby wailed loudly. He had forgotten about the child. He realised that it could not be left on its own; not with the jackal prowling around. Yet, by the same token, neither could the sheep be left untended.

While he hopped around in agitation, the woman's words about the child being more important than the sheep, haunted him. *Baas* Conrad was away, only *Misies* Henrika was home, and he dreaded the prospect of approaching her. He knew that there would be no end to her questions and if there were no answers she was quite capable of flying into a rage.

114

He was tempted to keep the watch and chain, but he knew that *Misies* Henrika would draw every detail out of him. If she discovered that he had tried to keep them, there would be no telling what she'd do to him. 'Hmm Ummmm,' he muttered, shaking his head. It wasn't worth the risk. Still it was a beautiful watch and he had seen how it glinted in the sun. Perhaps ... No ... Tollie wrestled with his conscience but in the end he decided to return it.

Having made up his mind, he hurried back for the baby, giving the prone figure of its mother a wide berth. With the baby in his arms, Tollie set off at a steady trot. He clutched the squirming infant to his chest and his long jacket trailed behind him, the ends flapping like the wings of a giant bird.

iGOLDIE

Treaty Kumalo's broad, flat, bare feet hugged the concrete pavement. Bewildered and frightened by the rush of early morning traffic she put a hand up to steady the roll of straw matting balanced on her head. Then very slowly and with infinite care, so as not to jostle the pedestrians with her awkward bundle, she turned her head. On the building behind her, in large, bold letters of gold, was the word SANLAM. She stared at it for a long time, puzzling over its meaning.

So this is *iGoldie*, she reflected with a little flutter of excitement. This was the City of Gold. But so far, apart from the lettering on the building, there was no gold anywhere in sight.

Treaty had trekked all the way from her village in the Valley of a Thousand Hills in Natal, to these bustling streets of Johannesburg to find her son, Nathaniel. From her pocket she withdrew the tattered letter, and cautiously opened it along the worn folds. Once again she studied the address.

The letter, almost five years old now, was from her son, Nathaniel. In it he described his job with a white family who lived in an enormous house in Houghton, a suburb of Johannesburg. The house, he said, was even bigger than the mission school she so often talked about. He and his wife lived in the servants' quarters behind the house. Each time Treaty read the letter she derived immense satisfaction from the knowledge that he was doing well.

When her husband died and the government started moving the villagers to the homeland, she decided that it was time for her to visit her son and his family. Except for the time

116

when as a young girl she had attended the mission school, she had never ventured too far from her village. The mission school was, in fact only about thirty miles east of her home, in a beautiful valley that sloped to the ocean.

So, in the staunch belief that she would have no trouble locating her son, Treaty had come to Jo'burg. Rolled in the straw mat, the ends secured with pieces of twine, were all her worldly possessions. Tucked under the crocheted skull-cap which she wore under her black turban was the last of her money. Ten one-rand notes. The rest, three rands in coin, knotted into a handkerchief and pinned to the inside of her bodice had been lost somewhere along the way.

On this journey to the city Treaty had worn her best clothes: a black serge skirt, white blouse, dark turban and a black shawl with long silky fringing. It was the uniform worn by the women of the church in the valley. For comfort's sake, she had removed her heavy black lace-up shoes and rolled them up in the shawl which she now wore tied around her waist.

Standing in the shade cast by the tall buildings, she felt the chill of morning air. Lifting her eyes, she searched the sky, and wondered how one could detect the passing of the seasons amidst buildings which obscured a view of the sun and the stars.

In the village each passing day, each week, each month, each year, left a clear and unmistakable sign that they had been and gone. Soon the wild flowers would bloom in the sheltered valleys of the Mgeni and the *veld* would be verdant. New life would abound; ants building hills as tall as huts and rainbirds calling, their fluted voices singing about the coming of the rain. In the valley the mist would creep along sending detached portions of itself scampering along the hillsides like sheep at play.

But it was all just memory now. The mission was no more. The government had taken the land also. They blamed the Africans for all the trouble.

'Too many cattle,' they said. 'It is destroying the land.'

117

She could see what they meant about the land being destroyed. It washed away in the rain forming deep cracks in the earth. Where the valley had once been green, its hills lush with matted grass, it now lay bald and scarred, the precious top-soil washed away by wind and water.

'This,' the men said, fixing them with angry glances, 'is due to the ignorance of the natives. Too many cattle,' they proclaimed. To correct the situation they returned with guns and shot the cattle.

'Anyone can see,' she told her husband, 'it is not a matter of too many cattle but too little land.'

In her mind's eye she saw again her husband's grave in the valley below the circle of huts, and in the distance the sound of children's voices raised in games and song.

Swaggering towards her along the pavement was a young boy, hands thrust deep into his pockets. Despite his youth and his swanky city clothes, there was a worn look about him, as though he had lived too long already. A passer-by threw a half-smoked cigarette into the gutter and she watched with astonishment when the boy stooped to retrieve it.

'*Umfaan*,' she said in the quiet maternal tone usually reserved for her sons and grandsons.

The boy ignored her. Puckering his lips around the cigarette he took a deep drag on the butt.

Undaunted, she continued: 'Can you tell me how to get to this place?' Carefully she opened the letter again, holding the parts together.

He removed the cigarette from his mouth and looked at her with eyes which already had the opaque gaze of an old man. He studied her with disconcerting insolence.

'Do you know the place?' she asked again.

He pushed his hat back a notch and continued to stare with those dead eyes. She felt a growing unease.

'What have you got in that mat?' he asked.

'Nothing,' she said, stepping back.

There was a menacing curl to his lips as he took a last long drag on the cigarette before flicking the stub into the gutter.

'Do you have money?' he asked.

'No.'

'Where are you from?'

She told him.

'You come from Natal and you have no money?' he said in disbelief.

'Can you help me?' she insisted.

He shook his head, thrust his hands back into his pocket and sauntered off.

She watched him amble down the street, stopping here to exchange a word, or there to elicit a laugh from cronies, who like him hung around street corners waiting for action.

An older man approached and she turned her hopeful attention to him. He glanced at the letter in her outstretched hand and she waited for his response, but his glance flitted into the distance and she knew with sinking heart that he was illiterate.

Another man thought he knew the place and told her to take the train there, but she could not understand the directions.

She repeated her question in English and asked him to speak slowly so that she could understand. But he was in a hurry and threw his hands up in exasperation.

'Can no one here speak Zulu?' she called after him.

The man hastened away.

For one fearful moment she was hemmed in on all sides by a crowd of people rushing across the street.

Treaty wandered aimlessly for hours. It seemed to her that no one cared. She trudged on, disheartened by the lack of compassion shown here.

Towards noon, hungry and exhausted but reluctant to spend any more of her dwindling resources, she sat down amidst the ruins of a building on Diagonal Street and buried her head in her hands. Will I ever find my way out of the city to my son's place, she wondered?

After a while she struggled to her feet, brushed the dirt from her skirt, picked up her roll and started off again. This time she chose a road at random and walked for some time without seeing anyone.

At length two African women approached, each staggering under an enormous burden carefully balanced on their heads.

'Can you direct me to a place called Houghton?' she asked.

The women exchanged pondering glances, one of them swaying unsteadily almost lost her load.

'Houghton? Let me see,' the one woman said, putting up her hand to scratch her head and withdrawing it again as she felt her load.

'No, I cannot, *Siesie*,' she said. 'Can you tell her what she wants to know?' she asked the other woman.

'Yes, I have heard of it,' answered her companion after long deliberation. 'But I do not know exactly where it is. I think it is there at the far end.' She pointed a bony finger in the direction from which Treaty had come.

'How far?' Treaty asked.

'A very long way, *Siesie*,' the woman replied, stabbing the air with her gnarled finger as if to place emphasis on the distance. 'Many miles,' she started to say, but when she saw Treaty's crestfallen expression, she stopped and gave a sympathetic smile instead. 'Be careful of the *tsotsis*, *Siesie*. They will steal from you and hurt you.'

Treaty thanked them and returned her burden to her head, wearily retracing her steps again. The mat, in spite of containing so little, grew heavier by the minute. It was a hot day and from time to time where she stopped to rest, she untied the turban and used it to blot the perspiration from her face before winding it around her head again and continuing on her way.

Eventually the road widened. It split and forked; other roads curled away from it and more came to intersect it, so that it was difficult to know whether to keep to the right or to the left. Now there were many more people and fleets of green buses filled to bursting.

The road that she was on led to a narrow street with a market which had many open stalls. Here were more crowds, jostling and pushing, all intent on their business. Now added to the congestion was a bewildering sea of cars, buses and bicycles, more than she had ever seen.

The noise was deafening and everywhere stall owners accosted passers-by, luring them in with promises of cheap prices and good quality. In the gutter dirty water had gathered in stagnant pools and the stench of rotting fruit and vegetables hung in the air.

This was no place to live, she thought ruefully. She should never have come here on her own. Occupied with these thoughts, she failed to heed the traffic signals and once or twice while crossing the street she was almost hit by a speeding car.

When a bus nearly ran over her at an intersection, the furious driver leaned out of his window and angrily shook his fist, shouting and cursing, forgetting that with the new spirit of liberalism he was not supposed to refer to her as a *kaffir meid*.

Eventually she escaped the congestion and turned into a side street. Here she found a quiet spot in a parking lot where she sat down beside an abutment, resting her head against the warm concrete block.

From across the street, the three youths who had been following her for several blocks bided their time. These were the *tsotsis*, the young thugs who were the scourge of the suburbs. They had identified her as being a simple country woman, lost and vulnerable in the big city. One of them carried a sharpened bicycle-spoke.

In the townships on pay day or when the elderly collected their meagre pensions, the *tsotsis* crept up on their victims grabbed them from behind and drove the spoke into the spine, severing the cord. They left their hapless victims dead or paralysed.

One of the youths had unsheathed the spoke from his trouser-leg and now held it in readiness as they stalked Treaty through the streets. Her circuitous route, however, led from one busy street to another and at each turn the opportunity for attack was lost.

They waited while she rested, for this again was not the appropriate place. There were still too many people around. Oblivious to the danger Treaty had fallen asleep, but she was rudely awakened by an indignant parking attendant.

'What are you doing here?' he demanded in Afrikaans.

In the English-speaking province of Natal the language of the Boers was rarely spoken and she did not understand a word of what he was saying. Bewildered, she gazed at the withered old man who confronted her, his dark beady eyes sunken into folds of loose parchment-like skin. He waited for her response, his eyes drawn into indignant slits.

'I was lost,' she explained in Zulu, but the man continued, ignoring her explanation. Hanging onto the abutment for support, she pulled herself to her feet and reached for her mat. Agitatedly he prodded her arm with a finger.

The young *tsotsis* called out to the man, baiting him, but he was too distracted by his attack on Treaty to bother about them. When the other attendants heard the commotion they came over to investigate. The old man now became even bolder and grabbed her arm, but she shook herself free, straightened her clothes and glared at him.

'This is a business place. It is not your bedroom,' he muttered in his alien language.

'I do not understand you,' she protested in Zulu. 'It is true what they say about the city. There is no kindness here.' She placed her mat on her head and stalked away while the man continued to chatter like a monkey. When she had put enough distance between them, she glanced back over her shoulder. He was still watching, shaking his fist at her. She hurried away.

At the corner she followed a crowd of people across the street against the traffic signal. It was the rush hour and the cars inched forward bumper-to-bumper. Everyone was in a hurry to get someplace. Yet getting anywhere was fraught with danger.

122

She decided to wait until the traffic had died down. The youths fell back, waiting. In that moment of calm decision she recognised them as the ones who had been shouting at the attendant at the car park. Perhaps they too, like her, were waiting for the traffic to die down.

The youths kept their distance, watching and waiting, their laughter exaggeratedly loud.

By the time the traffic had thinned out, some of the street lights had winked on, and the thought of finding her way around in the dark filled her with new dread. She was afraid now of continuing on in this place with its mountains of concrete and glass; its crowds and machines and grey streets battened down to the earth. How joyless it all was amidst the angry faces, all glaring, spitting and jostling.

Although she was unable to see the sun going down, she caught its fading rays glancing off the glass façades. It reminded her of the ocean on a summer's afternoon, the tall grass waving sinuously in the breeze; huts and *kraals* built on the slopes seeming almost to tumble down the hill towards the ocean.

There was a chill in the air; Treaty untied her shawl and sat down on one of the marble steps to put on her shoes. She gathered the shawl about her shoulders, nervously glancing at the few people who still lingered in the front of the building.

The youths sidled closer and she finally began to suspect that they were up to no good. Was it a game they were playing or were they lost too? They looked so young, so ragged, much worse off than the children in the village. Then she saw a black man coming out of the building wearing a grey suit and carrying a black briefcase like the Whites who had left the building before him. The steady flow of people out of the building had dwindled to a few stragglers. She mustered her courage and approached him, greeting him in Zulu.

He paused just for a moment, irritated because he was anxious to get home. There were always hawkers in this neighbourhood, people selling their wares. The story about the streets being paved with gold was not exclusively a white man's myth. Unlike the other beggars there was a touch of pride in her bearing. She looked more like a church-goer than a beggar, but then he saw the suspicious bulge in the roll of matting – odd shapes, like crudely carved curios – and he pushed by.

She called out to him in Zulu.

'I don't want to buy anything,' he responded gruffly, hurrying along.

A little way behind her three dark shadows hesitated and then retreated as more people came out of the building. When a police car cruised by, the shadows slunk into a darkened alley. By this time the man had turned on his heel and was half-way down the block, and the shadows behind Treaty once again appeared scuttling ever closer. She hurried after the man, balancing her burden with one hand and waving the letter in the other. She fell in step beside him, pressing the letter into his hand.

'What is wrong with you, Auntie?' he asked brusquely.

She opened the letter and pointed at the address. 'Please tell me how to find this place,' she said in Zulu. 'It is the address of my son. How will I get there?' she asked. 'I do not know the city. I am from a village in Natal, from a place they call The Valley of a Thousand Hills.'

'You are a long way from home, Auntie,' he said, 'and this place of your son is a long way too. It is too far and too dangerous to walk there.'

'How will I get there?' she asked in dismay.

'How would I know?' he replied.

Treaty was crushed; disheartened she turned from him. 'Do you know anyone in the township?' he asked.

She shook her head, then with a wery sigh she thanked him. She lifted the mat back onto her head and dejectedly turned to go in the opposite direction. She did not know where she could go or where she would spend the night. But at that moment she was so tired that she didn't care. As the *tsotsis* crossed the street, the man saw them and shouted a warning that he would call the police. Although they taunted him with laughter, they came no closer.

He went on his way reluctant to get involved in someone else's troubles. Did he not have enough of his own? But he could not put her out of his mind; at the end of the block he turned to look back, but the woman had already rounded the corner, as had the youths who were following her.

Treaty trudged on. Although warned about all the dangers of a big city, it was difficult to relate to something she had not experienced before. Her desire to see her son and grand-children far outweighed any concerns she had about permits, police or *tsotsis*.

She could not imagine what it was like to go through life not trusting anyone. The world after all was made up of all sorts of people, both good and bad. The youths were still following, and she began to realise that she should have heeded the warnings about the *tsotsis*. But was it not silly to be afraid of children? She hurried along now, sticking to the well-lit streets, trying not to panic. The boys were coming closer, laughing and joshing amongst themselves. With their approach she sensed the overwhelming presence of evil.

'Oh God, my God, do not Thou forsake me. Yea, though I walk through the valley of the shadow of death, I shall fear no evil, if Thou art with me ... '

A hand tapped her shoulder. She gasped in fright almost dropping her mat. Slowly, with trembling limbs, she turned.

It was the man she had spoken to outside the building.

'Come with me. I will take you to that address,' he said.

Treaty looked over his shoulder and saw that the youths had fallen back. She had no choice but to go with him. She was caught between the devil and the deep blue sea. 'Lord, I give myself into your hands,' she muttered.

The man led the way, past tall buildings which cast shadows of darkness she had never experienced before.

'Have you eaten today?' he asked.

She shook her head. 'I am not hungry.'

The only belongings of any value were contained inside the

rolled up straw mat. Possessions that would be meaningless to a stranger. Who would want a Bible, a small cooking vessel that she had cherished all these years; an old hat that had belonged to her husband John – and his pipe, the one that she had bought for him when he became ill?

I have nothing, she thought, unless he knows about the ten rands I have hidden under my turban. Is my life worth that? I would gladly give it to him if that is all he wants. I cannot die now, not before I have seen my son and my grandsons.

'I have my car in the next block,' the man said over his shoulder, striding briskly ahead of her. He, too, was afraid of the *tsotsis*. He knew what they were capable of and kept an eye on them. Even though his presence had deterred them, they were still a danger.

Treaty followed, nervously glancing back over her shoulder too. When they reached the next block, they turned the corner and the man stopped beside an old beaten-up Morris Minor.

It seemed to Treaty that by some mysterious design the streets had emptied. The noise had died down and rows of lights climbed to the top of tall buildings where large signs flashed on and off.

'Come Auntie. If we don't hurry those *tsotsis* will be upon us.'

Across the street a light staggered on, illuminating the picture of a scantily dressed woman with long bare salmon-pink legs. A message flashed on beneath the sign but it was gone before Treaty could read it. The sign darkened again, then the whole process repeated itself once more. This time she was ready and her eyes pounced on the advertisement for stockings.

From an open doorway she caught the smell of fish and chips. It was rich and tempting, impossible to shut out. It trapped her, knotting her stomach and bringing with it waves of nausea which left her dizzy and light-headed.

'Give me the letter,' the man said. 'Let me see it again.'

She handed the letter to him.

'Uh, huh. Yes. I will take you there on my way home to Alexandria Township.'

The man waited for her to get in. He saw her swaying and reached for her outstretched hand. She saw him leaning forward but she couldn't move.

Suddenly everything blacked out and she slid onto the pavement. When she fell against the door, the handle caught her turban. The ten rands fell onto the pavement and a gust of wind swept them into the gutter.

Somehow the man managed to get her into the car and by the time Treaty came to, they were well on their way to Houghton. It took a long time and at one point it seemed that they were lost, but after a few turns the man seemed satisfied that they were on the right road. The houses were all big and she could not believe that in each of these lived only one family.

But this was so, the man insisted. All the homes and streets were so well lit that she could even see the trees. There were high fences and gates around the houses so that it was difficult to see them. The man scrutinised the street names while carefully negotiating his way between the parked cars.

'There it is!' he exclaimed, pointing to a street sign which read Hillside Place. 'Now look for number forty-two,' he instructed, peering at each gate as they slowly drove by.

'Here. Here it is,' Treaty cried halfway down the block, jabbing at the windscreen as they approached a large house with wrought-iron gates. 'It is here ... number forty-two.'

The man had passed by but he stopped and reversed back to the house. 'You are right, Auntie. This is the place.' He rolled down his window and for a moment sat staring at the gate. 'But how will we get in there?' he asked.

'We must find a way,' she said.

Thoughtfully the man reversed a little further in search of a side entrance. Finding none he swung the car around so that the lights shone on the main gate.

'There it is,' he cried. 'See Auntie it is a bell that we have to ring to call the people.' He got out of the car and pressed the buzzer.

There was a long pause and he pressed the buzzer again. From the grounds came the sound of dogs barking. The lights in the front of the house went on and he could see the curtains parting as someone peered out.

'Who is it?' a voice called through a small black box.

'Jo, Jo, Jo,' Treaty exclaimed in fright.

'Excuse me sir,' said the man. 'I have here the mother of Nathaniel Kumalo. She has come all the way from Natal to see her son.'

'He is not here. He doesn't work here any more,' a male voice answered gruffly.

'But please, sir, she ... '

'You heard me.'

The man stared at the box for a while, then looked at the house where the windows were lit. Dejectedly he turned back to the car. 'What will you do now?' he asked.

'I don't know, *buti*. I don't know.' Treaty's shoulders drooped and she sat staring at her hands in her lap. 'Out in the street when I fell, I lost all my money. I have nothing now, not a penny.'

'We had better go before they call the police. We will be in trouble for being here without papers.'

She nodded.

'Where will you go, Auntie? You do not have the papers to be in the township.'

Slowly Treaty glanced up and shrugged with weary indifference.

At that moment the lights in the grounds flashed on and the dogs, released from their pen, rushed to the gate barking furiously.

'We'd better go,' the man said starting the car.

'Wait,' Treaty said, putting her hand on his arm as a woman appeared at the gate.

'One moment,' the white woman shouted waving to attract their attention. Then she called out to the dogs, silencing them.

Treaty got out of the car and the man hurried after her.

'Are you Nathaniel's mother?' the white woman asked through the bars of the gate.

'Yes,' Treaty said.

'I'm sorry my husband spoke so harshly to you. I know you've come a long way.'

'Does Nathaniel still work for you, Madam?' asked the man, anxious to confirm this one point because there was still the problem of what to do with Treaty.

'No. He's no longer with us. But I know where he is.'

'Do you mean you have his address?' the man asked.

'Yes, it's not too far from here.'

'When did he leave?' Treaty enquired in a small nervous voice.

'A long time ago. Three years ago.'

For a moment Treaty looked perplexed.

'There was an accident,' the woman started to explain. 'My husband was backing out of the driveway and he didn't see Nathaniel's little boy playing behind the car. It was a terrible accident.' She paused, waiting for the words to sink in. 'Nathaniel left soon after. He works for another family, but it is too late to go there now. Here in the backyard is a spare room where you can sleep for tonight. Tomorrow you can see your son.'

The man breathed a sigh of relief.

'Thank you. Thank you so much.' Overcome with relief Treaty lapsed into Zulu. 'Thank you for bringing me here,' she said when the man handed her the mat.

'Walk carefully, Auntie,' he said.

'Thank you, *buti*. You too, and God bless you.' She watched him drive away and it occurred to her that she hadn't asked his name.

129

THE WORLD ACCORDING TO
MRS ANGELA RAMSBOTHAM

Mrs Ramsbotham was up early on Tuesday morning. Passing by the dresser-mirror she paused to peer at her image, probing the puffiness around her eyes. Then with an indifferent shrug she turned away from her reflection to stare out of the window.

Outside, the sun slowly climbed over the horizon. In the distance plumes of smoke curled against the red and indigo hues of the dusky sky. From the kitchen came sounds of life, indicating that Daniel, the houseboy, had arrived a little earlier than usual.

Mrs Ramsbotham turned away from the window and cast a long resentful look at her husband's sleeping form before getting into the shower. Under the sharp needle-like sting of the water, her mind began to function. With characteristic fussiness, she once again reviewed the schedule for that day.

It was with great relief that she realised the major task had been accomplished. The house with the help of extra staff was immaculate. Everything from glassware to silver sparkled in readiness for the dinner party. Things were under control. There was no reason to worry. In an effort to dispel a nagging feeling of unease, she shut her eyes and lifted her face and her sagging breasts to the jets of water – offering herself in a sacrificial way to the Gods of Dinner Parties.

Despite all the preparations, and all the contingency arrangements made for this all-important party, she could not shake off her premonition of impending disaster.

Wearing her comfortable old terry dressing-gown she went downstairs to take her morning tea on the porch. It was still early and the bright morning sun was just brimming over the horizon. For a moment she stood against the rail of the porch, her critical glance taking in every detail of the grounds all the way down to where the high stone wall was topped by two rows of barbed wire.

The hydrangea, hibiscus, and bougainvillaea bushes splashed vivid colours against the green of the freshly mowed lawns. To the right of the flagged pathway and visible from the wide veranda which ran the length of the house, was the swimming-pool. At the far side, a gravel driveway curved towards a large wrought-iron gate which was generally locked.

The gate, like a dam wall, stemmed the tide of change. Since Independence the straggling township, replete with beer parlours and unsightly hoardings which advertised detergents, refrigerators, Vaseline and skin-lightening creams, was encroaching on the Ramsbotham estate. Not only did the mushrooming township bring its unsavoury characters to her gate and into this once exclusive neighbourhood, but it also brought with it the biggest blight on the landscape: a roadside market stretching about half-a-mile down the road.

Daniel appeared like a ghost on the porch, quietly setting down the tea tray on the rattan table. Mrs Ramsbotham acknowledged him with a nod of her head and he turned to leave. But before he could go any further she stopped him in his tracks. 'Why is the wheelbarrow still over there?' she demanded, pointing to where the gardener had left it.

'I don't know, Madam,' Daniel replied, one bare foot already halfway across the threshold, the other hovering just behind it.

'Your cousin is my garden boy. You brought him here to work. He is your responsibility,' she told him.

This didn't make much sense to him, but he wasn't going to argue with her. Instead he lowered his glance and became invisible. It always worked, just like the magician's trick he had once seen at a show in the township hall.

Mrs Ramsbotham glowered impatiently, but it was useless, she knew that those opaque orbs had turned inward and nothing she said would make any further impact on him. 'Will you please make sure that it is put away. And while you're at it, you might remove the leaves floating in the pool.'

He said nothing. Just stood there with his head bowed.

'Daniel,' she said sharply. 'Did you hear me?'

'Yes, Madam,' he answered, finally raising his head.

Satisfied that she had at last got a response out of him, she turned away and missed seeing the resentment in his yellow eyes.

Quickly then, in case she changed her mind, Daniel's other foot followed the first across the threshold.

At the far end of the driveway a lorry passed by, the drone of voices and raucous laughter shattering the peaceful morning air. A pall of blue smoke drifted in from the township forming a dark haze over the area.

Mrs Ramsbotham had almost finished her tea when her husband joined her. She was still annoyed with him. He had shown a surprising lack of consideration by inviting an Indian couple to tea that day when she still had so many details to take care of for the dinner that evening.

It was hard to forgive his lack of sensitivity. All night long she had fumed, rehashing the old arguments. She recalled the times when she had muddled through; occasions when he had, without prior notice, brought home guests for dinner. This time, however, he had gone too far. He was taking her for granted and she was not having it. He is spoilt, that's his trouble, she concluded. I've spoilt him.

'You know, my dear,' Mr Ramsbotham said, settling back into the rattan chair with his cup, 'I think the electronics dealership is a jolly good idea. With sanctions against the Republic things are going to be rather tight all round. I can see all sorts of opportunities. If only I can get that franchise.' He paused, his eyes narrowing thoughtfully.

She knew that this was his way of trying to get round her to have the Indian couple for morning tea. But there was no way she was going to give into him on this issue. This was one time she would put her foot down. There was just so much anyone should be expected to cope with. 'I don't want to hear one more word about the Indian couple coming to tea,' she stated firmly.

'But I can't cancel it just like that,' he said snapping his fingers. 'What will they think of me?'

'That's your problem.'

'It's all in the interest of business.' His moustache twitched. He could feel the tic of irritation in his upper lip and his hand went up to stroke and twirl his moustache. 'The fellow will be leaving for Tokyo tomorrow afternoon.'

'How on earth do you expect me to cope with everything?' she demanded. 'We have all these people coming for dinner tonight. People who are important to our position in the community.'

'Yes, indeed,' Mr Ramsbotham continued, stroking his moustache.

'I have enough on my plate as it is. I will not sit here listening to you going on about your outrageous business plans.'

He opened his mouth to protest.

'Not another word,' she warned, raising a finger.

He fell silent and after a long moment asked: 'Who have you invited?'

'I've told you about it,' she replied, but with a long-suffering sigh repeated it all again. 'The Patons are coming and the Moores; Charlotte Ryan, that nice young woman from the Republic who's teaching at the university; Michael Shedd, he's that handsome young man from the High Commissioner's Office,' she said ticking the guests off her fingers. 'I do so hope that they like each other. Of course the American Ambassador and his wife are coming as well. I've been dying to meet them.' Her grey eyes moved distractedly to a point in the distance. 'I want everything to be perfect for this evening's occasion. I've hired two maids to help with the preparation of the meal and the serving. I expect them to be here around three o' clock. They came highly recommended by Jennifer Snowdon who does a great deal of entertaining. There was just no way that I could possibly manage with Daniel alone. You know how doltish he is.'

'He's not that bad,' her husband interjected.

'Oh, you have no idea.'

'Well, I'm sure everything will work out fine, my dear.'

'Will you see to it that the wheelbarrow is removed from the pathway? The garden boy left it out there.'

'Of course, I'll make sure that Daniel puts it out of sight. Looks like you have everything under control, dear,' Mr Ramsbotham observed. 'It might do you good to take a breather.'

She gave him a crushing glance.

But he wasn't easily subjugated. 'It's only for tea. One cup of tea. I promise they won't stay long,' he cajoled. 'It's important for my business. M.K. is a good contact. He's a bright chap. Has a Ph.D in computer science. I believe he spent some time in California. Apparently he's a product of Silicone Valley. He's quite a jolly chap really.' He leaned back in his chair, long legs stretched out, chin resting on the point of the steeple formed by his hands. 'This may be the opportunity I've been waiting for. He and I could go into partnership.'

'David!' his wife cried, dismayed.

'Purely business, my dear Angela. M.K.'s a good sort. Besides, he has contacts all over the world.'

'For heaven's sake, David. You're a reputable businessman. Why would you want to associate yourself ... and me ... with someone from a second-class trading area? You know what the stores are like on Manica Road. What about our reputation?'

'Rubbish, my dear. This is not the time to be snobbish. It's a jungle out there and we have to survive.'

Mrs Ramsbotham glowered at her husband.

'We've been through all this before and I'm not changing my mind about a partnership with M.K.'

'What is his name?' she asked coldly. 'I can't go through life calling him M.K.'

'He's one of the Patels.'

'Which one? Every second one of *them* is a Patel. What is his first name? At least if you insist on doing business with him, I ought to be able to distinguish him from the rest.'

134

He shrugged. 'Everyone calls him M.K.'

'How ridiculous,' she said crossly.

He smiled at her with an air of patronising indulgence then went into the house.

Mrs Ramsbotham remained on the veranda for some time after her husband had gone, but eventually she too drifted indoors. 'Daniel!' she called.

There was no response.

'Daniel!' she called again, finally going in search of him. She tracked him down in the kitchen. 'Daniel, I've been calling you. Did you not hear me?'

'No, Madam.' He was at the sink with his back to her.

'Have you made the bed in my room?'

'Yes, Madam.'

'I left the white bedspread out on the chair. Did you put it over the bed?'

'No, Madam.'

'Why on earth do you think I left it out on the chair?'

Daniel was silent, his back still stubbornly turned towards her, his grip tightening around the pot handle. After a night at the beer-hall, he was feeling tired and hung over. It was quite a feat keeping his temper in check, and he concentrated on cleaning the saucepan, scrubbing it so furiously that the steel pad disintegrated in his hands.

My name is not Daniel. I am Dynamite Nkala, he seethed to himself. He hated the name Daniel. It was a white man's name, and he hated this woman who treated him like a fool. To her he was no more than a child, a thirty-year-old *boy*. He had informed her on the day he started in her employ that he would not respond to Daniel.

'What kind of a name is Dynamite?' She had laughed at his indignation and had blithely continued to address him by the name of her choice.

She was rattling off a whole list of instructions: Do this, do that ... He yanked the plug out of the sink and turned on the tap to drown out the sound of her voice. He blocked her from his vision. Only the disembodied voice reached him, and that

135

too he would have liked to silence.

'You can do the laundry the day after tomorrow. From now on you'll have to do the washing by hand. I'm sick and tired of telling you that you cannot put colours with whites in the washing machine. Colours and whites don't mix.'

'You put the washing in last week, Madam,' he reminded her.

'Will you please stop arguing with me and finish off upstairs. Please remember to put the spread on the bed. And do be careful, I don't want your prints all over it.' She paused. 'On second thoughts,' she said as he was about to leave the kitchen, 'wear the gloves.'

Daniel's back straightened perceptibly.

'There's no point in being mulish about it. I insist.'

Daniel remained in the doorway.

'You'd better get used to it. From now on you'll be wearing them regularly.'

His eyes glazed over. He wondered what his cronies would think of him wearing white gloves. No doubt he'd be the joke of the township. 'Look!' they'd cry, 'there goes Dynamite Nkala, wearing white gloves like a trained monkey!'

She waited, hands on her hips.

Finally, he took a deep breath and marched over to the drawer where the gloves were kept. He removed a pair and slipped them on, keeping his eyes averted, for he knew that what he felt would be reflected there.

'See,' she said, 'there's nothing to it. Now remember when you put the spread over the bed, be sure that the fringe is even on either side. The pattern must be right in the centre, and fluff up the pillows before you tuck the spread under. I can't stand a bed that is lopsided.' She leaned to one side to emphasise her point. 'Do you understand what I mean?'

Daniel nodded.

'Good, I'll look in later to check. It's a very valuable heirloom and almost impossible to clean. I'm sure my guests would love to see it this evening.'

Daniel hurried away. His life had changed little since

Independence, he reflected as he climbed the stairs. No money. No jobs. Like the majority of Blacks, his expectations had been dashed. For years prior to Independence people at the beer-hall had talked about how they would prosper under a multi-racial government. Now they had independence but no prosperity.

Like others he had lost faith in the new government. The only contented people were the politicians who drove around in their black Mercedes-Benz cars. The rest of them were still poor and jobless, just as they had been during white rule. It didn't make any sense that they should still have nothing in a country that now belonged to them.

'Why can we not go out and take what we want?' They had argued about this at the beer-hall the previous night. 'After all it is our country.'

It was hard to stomach the inequity. On the one hand there were the politicians, on the other there were white people, and they were caught in the middle.

Mr Ramsbotham eventually gave in to his wife and telephoned M.K. He was put out and embarrassed about having to renege on a commitment, so he tried to make it up in another way.

'Something's come up M.K. I have to cancel tea.' There was a pause at the other end. 'But look, I have a better idea. We're having a dinner party tonight. Just a few people including the Ambassador and his wife. Why don't you and your wife join us? We'll get a chance to talk, I'm sure.'

Mrs Ramsbotham who was passing her husband's study at that moment, overheard this conversation.

'I'm terribly sorry to change plans, old chap, but try and make it, will you?'

Mrs Ramsbotham was positively livid with rage. 'How could you do such a stupid thing?' she demanded when he put the phone down.

'What do you mean?' he asked.

'Oh for God's sake,' she shouted. 'Are you so stupid? Can't you see what you've done? What on earth were you thinking of?'

137

For a moment Mr Ramsbotham was stupified by this attack. 'Settle down Angela,' he said. 'I'm sure our guests will understand.'

'Understand what?' she screamed at him.

'These people realise that sooner or later the old barriers between black and white have to come down. This is Zimbabwe now. It's no longer Southern Rhodesia,' he explained in a calm rational way. 'Please remember, also, when you're talking to others, Salisbury is now known as Harare.'

'Harare is a dirty little native township on the outskirts of the city,' she spat the words at him.

'Not any more,' he retorted. 'It's time for you to change your thinking, Angela. You can't hang onto the past forever. The reality is that we have a black government. Colonialism is an anachronism.'

Mrs Ramsbotham was too angry to continue. She turned on her heel and hurried away, afraid that she might say something that she'd regret later.

Fortunately for Mr Ramsbotham, later that afternoon M.K. Patel telephoned the Ramsbothams to decline the invitation to dinner. When Mrs Ramsbotham answered the phone, he explained that his wife had made prior arrangements for a family gathering.

Mrs Ramsbotham had never been so relieved about anything in her life as she was when she put that phone down.

By four o'clock the two maids had not yet put in an appearance. In the meantime, Daniel started the preparations in the kitchen. There was no hint at all about the fact that he had told the two women not to come. He was not going to be undermined any more. This was his territory. If anything was to be done here, he, Dynamite Nkala would do it.

Mrs Ramsbotham, a little frantic by this time, came down to help. The leg of lamb and the roast veal had been prepared and cooked ahead of time. All that was left to do was the preparation of the first course – the fowl.

In the kitchen she found Daniel busily cleaning and washing the Cornish hens she had set out on the counter.

'No. No, Daniel. These are delicate creatures. You must treat them gently or you'll tear their tiny limbs apart. Here, let me do it. Where are the bay leaves for the stuffing?' she asked.

Daniel shrugged.

'Find them,' she hissed through gritted teeth. Things were not going well. Where on earth were the maids, she wondered? They were supposed to be here ages ago in order to help with the preparation and cooking. How could she possibly trust such a task to Daniel?

When Mrs Ramsbotham phoned Jennifer Snowdon she was out but her houseboy told her that the maids had gone home.

'But they were supposed to come here?' she wailed.

'I don't know nothing, Madam,' he said and put the phone down.

'Wait a minute,' she cried. 'Can you get them back?'

But it was too late, he had already hung up.

She returned to the kitchen where Daniel was still searching through the cupboards for the bay leaves. He returned empty-handed.

'Now don't tell me you can't find them. How many times have I told you to organise the shelves?' she asked, a note of exasperation creeping into her voice. 'If you put all the bottles of herbs and spices together as I told you to do, we'd have no trouble finding anything, would we?'

Daniel ignored her and busied himself at the sink.

'I don't suppose there's any sense in wasting time looking for it. I'll get a fresh bottle from the pantry.'

Promptly at seven o'clock that evening their guests arrived and were met at the door by the hosts. This was one occasion when Mrs Ramsbotham regretted not having a liveried doorman. It would have gone well with the house, furniture and the atmosphere she had strived to create for the evening.

Cocktails were served in the impressively appointed front sitting-room, where many priceless antiques were on show.

The guests were naturally quite taken with what they saw and expressed their admiration. While the men gathered around the bar, the women bandied about such words as 'exquisite, remarkable, tasteful'. Mrs Ramsbotham lapped it all up; particularly flattering was the graciousness of the Ambassador's wife who was quite new to the country.

After a while the sherry and the compliments started having a heady effect and Mrs Ramsbotham relaxed, allowing herself to be swept along in the flow of conversation. For a while all the day's problems lost their significance and drifted away into the background where they languished, forgotten. It didn't matter now that the maids had let her down, she and Daniel hadn't done too badly. She had to admit that things were going very well indeed.

It occurred to her that if they were so impressed with the few pieces in the front room, how would they react to the superb dining-room suite with its enormous sideboard, intricately carved with mirrored insets. This was her pride and joy and she could hardly wait for their reaction. Mrs Ramsbotham lavished more time and attention on maintaining the furniture in this dry climate than she did on any of her family.

'You certainly have some lovely pieces, Mrs Ramsbotham,' the Ambassador's wife said to her at the first opportunity.

'Thank you,' Mrs Ramsbotham smiled, overcome by a delicious feeling of elation.

'Such lovely pieces.'

'It's taken many years to assemble it all. I started collecting antiques as a hobby, but it's much more than that now,' she said.

'It's an obsession,' her husband interjected from the far end of the room from where he had overheard this comment.

'The embroidery on these chairs is quite exquisite,' Mrs Moore added.

Mrs Ramsbotham positively glowed from the effects of the sherry now. 'Oh, my dear,' she exclaimed to Mrs Moore who had been to the house before and was quite familiar with the Ramsbotham home. 'You know that bedspread I was telling you about?'

'Yes, of course,' replied Mrs Moore. 'I've been waiting for ages to see it.'

'Well, I got it out of mothballs and I've placed it over my bed. Later, if you like, we can go upstairs to take a look at it.'

'I'd be delighted,' Mrs Moore responded with a disarming smile.

'What is this bedspread?' the Ambassador's wife asked.

'Oh, it's been in my family for almost a century now. The linen is handwoven, edged with a six-inch lace border, all hand-tatted of course by one of my ancestors. The centre piece is a delightful garden study in *petit point*, hand-stitched by Lady Carlisle,' she dropped the name casually, hoping that someone other than Mrs Moore would pick it up.

Mrs Paton obliged. 'Oh, I've heard of her. She was a very well-known artist in the 1800s.'

'Yes. Apparently she was quite close to my great-great-grandmother,' Mrs Ramsbotham added for the benefit of the Ambassador's wife.

'It must be quite magnificent and very valuable, I'm sure. I read that her embroidery has fetched a fortune. Actually I think I've seen some of it hanging in Westminster Abbey, and I do believe that there are a few pieces in the gallery at Buckingham Palace,' Mrs Paton said, leaving this statement open to interpretation.

Mrs Ramsbotham wanted to ask her whether she'd actually been to the Palace, but then thought that the question might not be an appropriate one at this time. She made a mental note, though, to pursue it at the first opportunity.

Charlotte Ryan listened in silence, wondering why on earth she had come. They were all so frightfully boring, except, of course, for the good-looking man from the High Commissioner's office.

Michael Shedd noticed her discomfort and moments later came over to rescue her.

141

Mrs Ramsbotham smiled, pleased that the two young people were displaying an interest in each other. She had hoped they would. It was good for their kind to stick together. There were too many of the Whites fraternising across the colour line, and all because they were lonely.

'Do you suppose we could see the bedspread?' Mrs Paton enquired. 'I'm dying of curiosity now,' she said.

'But of course, my dear. We'll go upstairs after dinner,' Mrs Ramsbotham replied. Things were really going quite well she decided, dismissing the reservations which had haunted her all day.

Daniel entered wearing white gloves and carrying a tray of canapes.

'Just set them over there, please Daniel. Thank you.'

He hesitated, head lowered, eyes flitting about nervously.

'You may go now,' she told him.

Daniel left the room.

'I see you have him wearing gloves,' Mrs Paton said. 'What a jolly good idea.'

'Yes, I never quite trust them with matters of hygiene you know.' She shuddered. 'It's their skin colour. It just never looks clean.'

'Have you ever thought of returning to England?' the Ambassador's wife asked in round-eyed innocence.

'Oh, yes. Things were truly dreadful after Independence. What with all of them taking over and wanting to move in everywhere. It was awful,' she sighed. 'Unfortunately David doesn't much care for the UK. You see he's spent most of his life here. The cold in England doesn't suit him very well. Besides,' she leaned forward conspiratorially, 'his business is here and he said he'd be damned if he was going to hand it all over to them. They've been terribly spoilt since independence. Won't do any work. It's as though they have a mental block when it comes to work. Take my houseboy for example ... '

'My dear Mrs Ramsbotham,' the Ambassador's wife interrupted, laughing, 'should you be calling a grown man *boy*?'

'We call them *houseboys*. Everyone does,' she explained.

'I see,' the Ambassador's wife glanced at her husband, who was listening to this exchange with a twinkle of amusement in his eyes. He had warned her about such dinner parties and he was pleased that she was holding her own so well. When no one was watching she signalled to him with an imperceptible arch of one brow. He smiled and then returned his attention to the conversation in his group.

'Well, I think we're just about ready for dinner now. Why don't you lead the way to the dining room, dear?' she said to her husband. 'I'll take a peek into the kitchen to make sure that everything is proceeding according to plan.'

Without the maids to serve at table, she would have to do most of it herself. Drat! she thought, but there was no other way. She was definitely not going to rely on Daniel to help with the serving.

The guests filed into the dining room where an admiring murmur went up about the dining-room suite and the table with its starched napery and sparkling silverware.

'I really can't wait to see Mrs Ramsbotham's bedspread,' said Mrs Moore to Mrs Paton.

'Neither can I,' the other replied.

They were about to sit down when there was a loud crash from the kitchen. The guests exchanged glances but politely refrained from comment.

'I'll just take a look to see what's happening,' Mr Ramsbotham said and excused himself.

In the kitchen he found his wife towering over Daniel like an avenging angel. Daniel was on his knees scraping together pieces of Cornish hen.

'What's happening here?' Mr Ramsbotham demanded.

'He dropped the hens!' she wailed. 'Oh David!' She was almost in tears now. 'My dinner is ruined. Absolutely ruined.'

'No, it isn't,' her husband said in calming tones. 'We'll make the best of what there is. You still have the lamb and the pork roast, and that's in addition to all the other little things that go with it. For heaven's sake Angela, you've been busy all day long. Surely you must have loads of stuff to feed them with? Skipping this one course is not going to be the end of the world.'

'You don't understand,' she moaned, covering her face with her hands.

'Of course I understand. I never much cared for the little blighters anyway.'

'I've just about had enough of you,' she shouted, turning on Daniel. 'Get your things. You're fired.'

'Don't be hasty my dear,' Mr Ramsbotham urged.

'No. He has to go. I will not have him in this house for one moment longer. OUT!' she cried in an imperious tone.

Daniel was still on his knees; their voices swirled above his head. He raised his glance and moved it from one face to the other. Then with tight-lipped dignity, he got up off his knees and stood upright. Without saying a word he removed his apron, tossed it into the sink, stepped over the mess on the floor and left the kitchen through the back door.

'Poor beggar,' Mr Ramsbotham said. 'I feel rather sorry for him.'

'I'm the one who needs your sympathy. I still have to feed our guests,' she said. 'What am I going to do?'

While the Ramsbothams argued, Daniel returned to the house through the front door. Very quietly he climbed the stairs to the master bedroom where the bedspread was perfectly aligned. Not a single crease or wrinkle marred the appearance of this exquisite piece of work.

He entered the room, pulled down his trousers and squatted on the bed; straddling the exquisite panel stitched by Lady Carlisle, he defecated.

Then as quietly as he had come, he departed, hurrying to the gate where he melted into the darkness beyond.

The Ramsbothams were still in the kitchen discussing their options. 'Let me do that,' Mr Ramsbotham offered, taking the dustpan and brush from his wife, and sweeping up the pieces of Cornish hen.

'I can't go back in there like this,' she said. 'I think what we should do is call Elise Collins. I know she won't hesitate to help. You call her dear, explain briefly what the emergency is and ask her please to dispatch her servants over here immediately. In the meantime I'll explain to our guests that we've had a bit of setback and that dinner will be delayed for about half-an-hour until Elise's servants get here. No doubt they'll understand,' she said, but without much conviction. Her voice quivered and it was only due to a supreme effort that she managed to maintain her composure.

'It's all right dear, we'll manage somehow. I'll see what I can do,' soothed Mr Ramsbotham.

'Darling,' she said, 'if you could only steer the men back into the living room for a few more cocktails, I'll take the ladies upstairs to see the bedspread.'

SEEDS OF DISCONTENT

The rain came down in torrents from a noon sky as black as night. The heavens groaned and heaved spewing jagged forks of lightning. We (a group of fifteen women and I) had been keeping a silent vigil on the city hall steps. When the storm broke we rushed for shelter, our placards and banners abandoned in a limp pile.

During a brief lull I dashed over to where a small group of protesters huddled beneath a marble overhang at a department-store entrance. I had barely reached this shelter when the heavens opened with a vengeance. In a matter of moments water cascaded over the flat overhang.

I leaned against the door, removed my shoes and emptied them of water, shook the runnels from my bright yellow plastic raincoat, secured the belt and waited along with the others for the storm to abate.

When the rain eventually eased off I hurried across the street. My car was parked two blocks away. Already I was drenched to the skin, my thighs chaffing in my soaked clothes. All of this to protest about the death of a woman who, until a little more than two years ago, I had not even heard of.

If anyone had told me a year or so ago that today I, Kathleen Stewart, would be out here in the rain participating in a political rally, I would have laughed at such absurdity. Yet here I am. It seems that once in a while something or someone passes through one's life (sometimes in an unobtrusive way) and after that nothing is ever the same again. That was the effect Celina had had on my life.

Earlier today a passer-by had stopped to give me a piece of her mind, sternly advising me that I ought to be ashamed of making such a spectacle of myself.

'That girl's a terrorist. She deserved what she got,' she said. 'Why don't you all go home?' Then shaking her head disgustedly she walked off with a parting shot: 'Thanks to people like you, we'll all end up being coffee-coloured someday.'

The absurd notion had crossed my mind as I glanced at the stormy sky, that this woman might have placed a hex on us.

My daughter, Beth, has just turned twenty-three. I'm fortyish – a solid and predictable type not much given to impulses. This could be substantiated by the fact that I've worked as a secretary with the same law firm for the past twenty years. I wear this kind of predictability like an old, comfortable coat, nestling into its warmth for security. But I enjoy my work and apart from the occasional black client, I never had much to do with non-Whites. Naturally there were servants at home but that is a different matter all together.

Looking back now I realise how much I've changed in the past three years. A process accelerated in the last eight months with the start of Celina's trial. (But more about that later.)

It's funny how life sometimes springs little surprises on you, (almost as if to jolt you out of your complacency); when at other times you can go full circle without as much as a ripple on the surface of your existence. I never allowed anything to disturb the tranquillity of my life; politics or the inequities of our system were of no consequence. Why spread seeds of discontent? As far as I was concerned the system worked; if it worked why bother to fix it? Except of course that my daughter was gradually whittling away at my attitudes, and would from time to time stand back, like a woodcarver, patiently assessing the results of her work.

She teases me about those early days. But actually the change had crept over me as subtly as a sunrise. Once when Beth was with me, I had occasion to cut an Afrikaner store clerk down to size because she had made some inappropriate and disparaging remark about a black woman who was ahead

147

of us at a check-out counter. Although Beth didn't say anything she did seem a little taken aback by my reaction. For a moment the startled cashier, red with embarrassment, glared at me before her face returned to its customary surly expression.

This incident, only one of the many that followed, had left me with a feeling of satisfaction, particularly when I saw the gleam in Beth's eye as we left the store.

How little I knew about my own daughter. It was only two years ago that I discovered the extent of her political involvement. Of course there had been a few early clues gleaned from her visits home and the obligatory telephone calls, but it was easier to ignore them. So, while I pretended that Beth was applying herself conscientiously to a degree in fine arts which she hoped would eventually lead her to a course in journalism, she was becoming a student activist adept at dodging tear-gas canisters.

Beth gave me the impression that she had many friends. There were always phone calls for her when she was at home. Although I never met any of her friends, she often talked about them. They were all mysterious, shadowy figures remaining like silhouettes against a darkening sky. Of course, like a typical parent, my main concern hinged around the availability of drugs on campus. At that particular point I wasn't overly concerned about her involvement in politics. I assumed that this was a phase which all students went through while at college.

In retrospect I realise how much I had under-estimated her. I was still thinking of her in terms of a sullen, rebellious teenager. Yet this phase had, without my being aware of it, given way to a new and ardent idealism. Instead of the once familiar monosyllables, her conversation now was articulate and peppered with *radicalese*.

My ignorance about my daughter was never more obvious than the time, about two years ago, when Beth phoned to say that she was bringing a girl-friend home for the weekend. I,

148

naturally, was quite delighted at the prospect of meeting one of her friends.

'That would be very nice,' I told her over the phone. 'Should I prepare the spare room?'

'No, don't go to any trouble. She can share my room. We'll be there around dinner time.'

When I heard the car pulling up, I hurried to the front door to greet them. I couldn't hide my shock and consternation when I opened the door to find a black girl on my doorstep. I was even more startled to discover how familiar and comfortable her relationship was with my daughter.

'Celina this is my Mum. Mum this is Celina.' For Beth it seemed the most natural thing in the world. After the initial shock I got a good grip on myself and set my face into a welcoming smile.

I took Celina's proferred hand and said: 'How do you do,' or words to that effect.

'Here give me your togs, Celina. I'll take them upstairs,' Beth said.

'I'll come with you.' Celina's eyes were like those of a trapped animal, anxiously searching for an escape.

Later while Celina was upstairs I cornered Beth in the kitchen. 'That was a rotten thing to do,' I hissed.

'You mean bringing Celina home?' she asked with infuriating innocence.

'No, you know what I mean. Not warning me that she's black.'

'I didn't think it was necessary,' she answered in that direct way of hers.

'It could have been a lot more embarrassing,' I scolded. 'Especially for her.'

There was an amused glint in her eyes as she said: 'You did very well.'

'I don't know whether to thank you or spank you.'

'Isn't she smashing though?'

I had to admit that she was indeed striking, almost regal in her bearing, with finely chiselled features. 'I don't ever want

149

you to put me in such an awkward position again,' I warned her.

I had prepared a roast leg of mutton with all the trimmings because this was Beth's favourite dish, but now I worried that under the circumstances this might not be appropriate. What do they eat I fretted? I knew that Lisbet, my maid, usually cooked mealie-meal pap, a stiff porridge. Should I prepare some of this? I was mortified when Beth made a joke about this at dinner.

Celina chuckled and there was no malice in her response when she said: 'The last time I had mealie-pap was on the farm when I visited my parents a year ago.'

'Where are you from?'

'A farm near Alice.'

She waited for me to ask where this was but I knew the Eastern Cape. My cousin lived in Grahamstown and we once drove out that way when we visited East London. In fact we toured quite a large area of the Ciskei.

'I've been to Alice,' I said.

Her surprise turned to delight and she smiled, making a face at Beth.

'You didn't tell me that you were there,' Beth teased.

'You didn't ask.'

We bantered back and forth like this and then I said: 'I don't understand why you've come all the way to Wits when Fort Hare is so handy. I've been told that it's quite a good university.' I refrained from adding 'for Blacks'. My cousins had told me that many black politicians, not only from this country but from neighbouring countries as well, had graduated from this university.

'I started my degree there but there were troubles. It's not what it used to be and my family thought it would be much better for me here at Witwatersrand University.'

By this time it was not only curiosity but a genuine interest that prompted my questions. 'What sort of trouble?'

'Mum, don't you read the papers?' Beth asked with a touch of impatience. 'It's more like a tribal college now.'

150

'Those people they were ruthless. They broke the spirit of the students and the staff,' Celina said.

'Who's *they*?' I asked.

'The government.' Celina lowered her eyes and fell into a thoughtful silence.

'That's why you left?'

She nodded, toying with her food. She sat with her arms on the table, slim shoulders haunched. 'My uncle, he used to lecture there many years ago. It was he who was instrumental in getting me transferred here. It has been much better, of course, for my education, but I think sometimes there are other things more important than that.'

There was a marvellous lilt in her voice. She had the same throaty quality I'd noticed in some of the African singers, whose voices had a depth and timbre that I had not heard elsewhere. It was quite a delight listening to her.

Later that evening I heard her and Beth singing in the parlour. I went to investigate and realised that they were singing *Nkosi sikelel' i Afrika*. I knew that this was the anthem of the African National Congress and I wasn't too thrilled about them singing it in my home. But their voices blended together so well that I couldn't help listening to them.

Beth noticed the look of concern on my face. 'Mum it's a beautiful song. I know what others have said, but it has nothing to do with racial hatred.'

'The fact is that these words are full of piety and respect for this country and its people,' Celina told me.

'*Nkosi sikelel'i Afrika* means *Lord Bless Africa*. Right Celina?'

The other girl nodded. '*May her horn rise high up;/Hear our prayers and bless us.*'

But I remained sceptical.

The weekend went well despite a few things which left me uncomfortable: like the two of them sharing Beth's double bed. This was probably the hardest thing of all for me to accept that first night. During and after dinner I had come to terms with the fact that she would be in the house for the

151

weekend. I had prepared the spare bedroom and had probably even made an unconscious note to wash the bedding separately. Had Celina been one of us, there would have been no problem; after all I was young once too and I know what fun it is to girl-talk about boys all night long. But what could the two of them possibly have in common, I wondered, as I listened to the giggling and the suppressed laughter?

I peeked in on them once during the night when everything was silent. They were fast asleep, Celina's arm flung across Beth's neck. There was an innocence about this scene which reminded me of two young play-weary children.

Because I had given the servant the weekend off when she came in early on Saturday morning, I ended up having to do most of the housework myself.

'What did you do a silly thing like that for?' Beth complained when she got up later and found that she had to help with the dishes.

'I didn't want her to see Celina here. It might give her the wrong idea,' I explained.

By Sunday I realised how foolish I had been. The fact was that I had thoroughly enjoyed having both of them home for the weekend. In between doing the dishes and what have you, I had even picked up a few words of Xhosa which Celina had taken great delight in passing on. Before they went I invited her back for another visit.

They left on Sunday night around eight o'clock. I saw them to the door and Beth gave me a quick hug and a kiss. 'See you again, Mum,' she said.

Celina leaned forward and I offered my cheek, but she caught me in a quick impulsive embrace: 'See you again, Mum.'

It dawned on me that I could no longer hide my head in the sand like the proverbial ostrich. I finally had to admit that Beth was 'involved' and as such she was exposed to a very real danger. But what could I do? She wouldn't listen to me, and I couldn't deal with her radicalism. I just wasn't equipped to fight it. My own indifference to politics had left me sorely ill-prepared. In the past, whenever we had argued about issues, our philosophies ran like two parallel tracks.

I never saw Celina again. I enquired about her a few times but Beth seemed vague about the girl's whereabouts. Then one day in the summer following Celina's weekend with us, Beth and I were sitting out in the shade of the gnarled, old pear tree. It was a typical summer's day. At ten o'clock temperatures had already soared into the mid-thirties. The flowers were in full bloom and there was a heavy silence in the air, disturbed only by the lazy drone of insects flitting between the beds where petals dropped from plants wilting in the hot sun.

Quite unexpectedly, as if choking on her thoughts, Beth suddenly said: 'We're white, Mum. What do we know about suffering? We're privileged by virtue of our colour, not because we've earned it. What have we done to deserve all of this?'

Surprised, I asked: 'What are you talking about?'

'It's just the way things keep happening. Things that make you wonder who you really are, and what life is all about.'

I waited, still not sure what had prompted this outburst.

'We think something's happened to Celina.'

'Why?'

'She's disappeared. No one knows where she is. Just vanished off the face of the earth. I'm sure it has to do with the explosion at the railway station three months ago.'

'Nonsense,' I said. 'Perhaps she's gone back to visit her parents in the village.'

'Or been killed by the police.' She sighed and glanced away.

'Have you tried giving her a ring?'

She laughed dryly. 'I don't think her parents would have a telephone.'

'Someone at Fort Hare might know,' I suggested.

She shook her head. 'Sometimes I think I'm the wrong colour.'

153

Squinting at her in the bright sunlight I said: 'Don't be ridiculous. We can't take the blame for everything just because we're white. What does that have to do with the fact that you can't reach Celina?'

'We are to blame.' Distracted for a moment, she toyed with a piece of twig that had dropped into her lap. '*We* started this whole mess. *We* separated people and emphasised their differences.'

'I worry about you Beth. I just wish you would show enough interest in your studies to finish your Master's and get started on a career. Ever since your father died ... '

She rolled her eyes. 'Not now, Mum.'

'No, please give me a hearing.' I put up my hand to silence her. 'I spend sleepless nights worrying about you and your safety. I wake up in a cold sweat in the middle of the night. When that phone rings, my heart stops. Do you know what this is doing to me?'

She was silent for a while, staring past me, then she said: 'Think about how a black parent feels. At least we go to bed at night, safely tucked in between clean sheets and a warm blanket. When we turn that light off, generally it's to have a good night's sleep. We don't have to rummage through refuse bins to find food, or have to worry about being raided at night, or live with the fear that we may never see our loved ones again.'

My patience snapped. 'Look,' I said. 'I don't deny that there are shortcomings in this system, but what do you think will happen when what we have breaks down? If we yield to pressure now we'll be swept away like matchsticks in a flood. You can't expect change overnight. Look what we've done for this country. Where would the Blacks be today without us?'

She returned to Jo'burg two days later, saying that she wanted to spend a couple days with friends before starting classes. The realisation that there were probably thousands of other parents going through the same anguish, didn't make it any easier for me. Why couldn't she just get on with her studies and stay away from the confrontations? It wasn't her affair, I thought, sitting on the edge of the bed while I watched her packing her small suitcase.

This all brings me to the trial and to the point where my life was jarred out of its placid orbit.

I had just gone to Grahamstown in order to spend a few weeks' holiday with my cousin. It was during the period when all the violent student clashes and protests were going on. It came as rather a shock when I discovered that the student unrest was spreading to other university campuses as well, including Witwatersrand University in Johannesburg where a student march had been disrupted by police using tear-gas and dogs.

There were reports of several injuries and arrests and I was nearly out of my mind with worry about Beth.

'She's old enough to take care of herself,' my cousin said, but any attempts to reassure me failed. Beth was my only child and I knew that she would be in the thick of things. For a week I tried unsuccessfully to get hold of her. I telephoned my friends, her friends and whomever else I could think of, but no one had heard from her or seen her recently. When I could bear it no longer, I returned home on the first available flight.

On the plane I scanned the *Sunday Times* but there was little news about the confrontations. Instead the front page was devoted to the trial, due to open in Pretoria on Thursday, of a dozen detainees who were facing various indictments under the Terrorism Act. The article referred to a countrywide organisation aimed at urban terrorism. The only woman named in the article was Celina Msimangu. It took a few moments for me to associate the Celina Msimangu described as a terrorist in the article, with the person who had spent the weekend at our place.

Apparently the young woman's capture had been a well-kept secret. She had been held incommunicado since her arrest five months earlier when she had been caught trying to escape to England. According to the article she was being charged as an accomplice in the railway-station bombing in which three Whites were killed. It was then that I remembered the conversation with Beth that day under the pear tree.

For the rest of the flight I was completely absorbed in all these thoughts. I recalled some of the details of the bombing, and the subsequent warnings from the government about a new wave of terrorism sweeping the country. All of this had happened prior to censorship and the newspapers had been filled with new and frightening speculations. It was hard to imagine that I had once viewed censorship with relief. For me it had been one way of ending the constant barrage of reports about trouble in the townships! Articles which I thought only served to feed our fears and insecurities. While others complained about the lack of civil liberties, I was relieved that the police were able to maintain law and order. The thought of social chaos filled me with dread.

Under pressure I might have subscribed to a transfer of power from Whites to Blacks, provided this was done through an orderly process, when of course the Blacks were ready. (This posture was the antithesis of what my daughter believed. She claimed that there would never be a voluntary transfer of power; that the white man is not interested in giving up or sharing power with the Blacks.)

When my flight arrived at Jan Smuts I was anxious to get home. My suitcase weighed a ton and I regretted that I hadn't brought the set of luggage wheels with me. I struggled away from the luggage carousel and finally managed to drag the heavy bag into the terminal, where I hailed a coloured porter who sidled over in a desultory manner. There will be no containing them if they ever get power, I reflected crossly.

He seemed to be caught in the indecision of whether to take my luggage or that of a male passenger. In weighing up the odds of possibly getting a bigger tip from the man, however, he was too long in making up his mind and another porter rushed to the assistance of this passenger. With exaggerated resignation the coloured porter lifted my luggage onto his trolley.

156

I arrived home at about noon and immediately set about tracing Beth. To my relief I eventually located her through a network of friends.

'I'm coming home for the holidays, Mum,' she said despondently and I guessed that the trial was occupying her thoughts.

Beth arrived late on Wednesday night and we talked away into the early hours of the morning. I learnt about the horrifying events that had occurred on campus when police had attacked an ostensibly peaceful march. When the conversation turned to Celina and the trial Beth's eyes filled with tears. I realised with a sense of shock that there were still many facets to this young woman that I knew nothing about.

I shared a rare closeness with my daughter that night. The conversation and her unburdening drew us together. We reminisced about the weekend she had brought Celina home. We laughed about the way she and I had done all the housework because I had given the maid the weekend off, and the way Celina had impulsively embraced me and called me Mum. Not only did we laugh together, we also cried about things that had affected us deeply.

A week later, just before the trial opened, I happened to be at the court-house picking up documents for one of the senior lawyers. I was preoccupied and wasn't paying much attention to what was going on around me. Suddenly I heard someone saying: 'Mum.' I glanced up. It was Celina. I was too startled to react. I merely stood there numb with shock while the police roughly nudged her past. She was thin and gaunt, not at all as I remembered her. In addition, she was manacled and wearing clumsy, ill-fitting prison garb. The only recognisable feature about her were her eyes: beautiful, large and doe-like.

When I finally collected myself it was too late. She had gone.

The shock of seeing her had left me rooted to the spot. What could she possibly have thought of me? All I could think of as I returned to the office was that quiet, plaintive 'Mum'. If that wasn't a cry for help, I don't know what was. Oh God, how awful!

I phoned Beth and related the incident. 'I was so upset, so horribly distressed at seeing her like that,' I said, 'that I couldn't say anything to her.'

There was a long silence at the other end of the phone. 'It's all right, Mum. I'm sure Celina understood,' she finally said.

On the Thursday, around noon, Beth and I were amongst the crowd waiting outside the court room. We were only there for about half an hour when the proceedings were adjourned. I was standing quite close to the door when the prisoners were escorted to a van for transfer back to the jail.

As they left the court-house, the crowd started singing *Nkosi sikelel'i Afrika*. I was about an arm's length from her. She seemed so calm; so resigned to her fate. A little shudder, some undefinable feeling, crept over me. Without even realising that I knew the words, my lips moved in accompaniment. She glanced at me as she passed. I could see in her eyes that she had recognised me.

'Celina … ' I said.

She turned. 'Mum?'

I smiled encouragingly and held out my hand, but they moved her along.

An African woman dressed in a black skirt, jacket and beret led the singing. Her voice, so forceful, so clear and defiant, conveyed a commitment and a devotion which made me realise for the first time that Beth probably had a better sense of this country than I had. I was still restricted and encumbered by all the old hang-ups about colour and superiority.

Despite the censorship during the weeks and months of the trial, one still got an idea of the terrible conditions endured by the detainees. The deprivation, the isolation and the constant torture to get confessions. No wonder, I thought indignantly, that some of them had actually caved in and had turned State witness.

'Does this now give you some inkling of what's really going on in this country?' Beth asked one day when she phoned. These days we spoke about nothing else but the trial.

Up to this point the victims of our system had all been faceless and anonymous. But now it was different. It had touched me in a very personal way through a young woman who could not have been much older than Beth. I thought of Beth there in her place and I was gripped by a cold panic.

I was at the court-house as often as I could be during the trial. Some days the court-room was jammed. I stood outside with the others, singing *Nkosi sikelel'i Afrika*.

If this had happened at some previous time in my life, I would have thought of myself as an innocent bystander swept up in the momentary drama of someone else's life. But I realise now that there are no innocent bystanders. We are all part of the fabric of this country, and whether we like it or not the responsibility for the ultimate outcome lies in our hands.

On the last day of the trial, I waited outside with more than a hundred people. The court-room was packed and on several occasions, the judge had asked for the court to be cleared because of repeated disturbances from the spectators' gallery.

In the end Celina and three others accused were indicted on five counts of terrorism, each receiving a sentence of life imprisonment. Three other detainees were given fifteen years each. Two received lesser sentences of ten years each. The man who had turned State witness received a six-months suspended sentence.

I was waiting outside, along with the rest of the crowd. Her parents and two of her sisters met her at the door. Her father was a frail, grey-haired man. Her mother wore a long black skirt and blouse, the traditional African dress. From their appearance one could see that they were poor and that they had probably sacrificed a great deal to put her through university. Now this! Although a little on the emaciated side, her mother was tall and stately and I could see where Celina got her proud carriage from. Her two sisters were sobbing. A hush fell over the crowd as the family took their leave of her.

159

My heart contracted painfully, I felt their anguish. I was a parent too.

She smiled at the crowd and I noticed a softening of her eyes. They were large and lustrous with a childlike vulnerability that touched me to the quick. The police officer prodded her roughly and in that moment that vulnerability was replaced by the old hardness, a defiance that suggested nothing could affect her any more. She gave the clenched fist salute and shouted *Amandla*. The crowd responded.

It was August. The trial had taken eight months. It was now about eight months since I had bumped into her at the court-house that morning. Two weeks later she was dead.

The rain was still beating down. At the newspaper stand across the street a soggy headline banner had come undone, dragging in a pool on the sidewalk. PRISONER JUMPS TO HER DEATH DURING INTERROGATION! Water dripped off the large red-lettered banner like blood from a wound.

According to the spokesman for the police, she had leaped to her death from the eighth floor of the Security Police headquarters while being interrogated by two officers. He claimed that her action had taken both officers by surprise and that they were unable to stop her in time.

In conclusion the spokesman added that the whole incident had been unfortunate and regrettable. That was the official version. I turned the corner, the headline still trapped in my peripheral vision.

There were counter-charges that her interrogators, after torturing her, had pushed her to her death. There were of course no witnesses to corroborate either of these stories. There never were any in the dark hours of the night when police interrogations ended in death.

I looked around for some of the protestors but most of them had vanished in the rain. All that remained were a few soggy placards dropped in haste. One of these lying face up read: YOUR CHILD COULD BE NEXT!

I could still see the headline banner as I climbed into my

car. For a moment I sat there watching the water whirl about the windscreen wipers. I wanted to get home so that I could phone Beth. I needed the reassurance that she was all right. I peered into the mirror, dabbing at the water with one of Beth's socks I had found on the back seat. I opened my window, poked my head out and eased into the traffic.

THE WOMAN IN GREEN

I was awakened from a deep sleep by a confusion of sounds. For a while I listened to the noise and the chatter of passengers hurrying by my window, then I sat up and drowsily peered at my watch. It was a few minutes before midnight. I rolled over in my bunk to squint through the slit between the wooden shutters. The sign at the railway station read 'Bloemfontein'.

The hissing and clanking of couplings, the screeching of wheels, the shrilling of a whistle and the mist-shrouded lights on the platform lent an air of eeriness to the scene outside.

I remained by the darkened window caught up in the atmosphere but then the whistled shrilled, rudely jolting me back to reality. The train jerked forward and just as I thought we were on our way, it abruptly screeched to a halt again. I noticed a commotion at the far end of the platform and inquisitively lowered the blind a few inches, craning my neck to see. A couple hurried into view. They appeared to be VIP's of some sort. I watched the woman who paused beneath the light standard. Her bearing and the atmosphere seemed to give her a quality of dislocation. Ensconced in the comfort of my bed, I felt a twinge of sympathy for the latecomers. I watched for a while longer until the group and their entourage passed beyond my line of vision.

Later the next morning, I saw the woman again, for the second time, at Park Station in Johannesburg, where the Cape Town Special sat on a branch-line awaiting a diesel engine. Eventually the engine arrived, reversed, grabbed the connection and jerked the carriages forward. The train heaved, the sudden motion throwing its unsuspecting passengers back against their seats.

I groped for my shoes, found them, but couldn't get them onto my swollen feet. I, obviously, was not going anywhere. I leaned back, propped my feet up on the radiator and absorbed in thought, stared out. Suddenly I heard high-pitched, girlish laughter. I thought I recognised the laugh and glanced up quickly. It was her, the same woman from the previous night, dressed in a gorgeous lime-green outfit. She hurried towards the train from the small bookstall where she had been browsing.

Last night too, they had almost missed the train at Bloemfontein. Some people were like that, I reflected wryly, always missing the boat or as in this case, the train. I watched as the man straightened his tie and buttoned his jacket, following a few steps behind her.

'Hurry, dear!' she called in Afrikaans, 'Or we'll be left behind.'

The train continued its slide along the track. Suddenly it braked with that screech of steel on steel that set one's teeth on edge. Although hampered by high heels, the woman broke into a run. Out of breath she stopped beneath my window in the second-class non-white carriage.

She had not yet noticed that she was being observed by me and placed one hand to her chest; with the other she pressed down her hat, a matching lime-green cloche. She was an attractive woman: tall, slim, and elegant looking. She was close enough for me to notice details; like the way her blouse was draped a bit daringly and pinned with a cameo. Even though I admired the simple elegance of her outfit, I knew that with my extra weight, the style would be quite unsuitable on me. I couldn't take my eyes off her. There was something so familiar about her. But for the life of me, I couldn't place her.

At that moment, while I was thinking about all this, she turned round, still wearing her smile. As she did so, her eye caught mine. She glanced at me, and there was a flicker of emotion in that look that I couldn't quite identify. At the same time the blood just seemed to drain right out of her face. It all happened very quickly. Her pallor, our glances meeting, her frozen smile. Then she hurried by. But in those split seconds my brain had registered her expression and I was perplexed. I cursed my bad memory for faces. Did I know her or did she merely remind me of someone I once knew?

For the next little while I could not shake her image from my mind. It haunted me. I was baffled. Who was this white woman in a green dress with dark brown hair and a laugh so distinctive and familiar that it had stirred a deep, subconscious memory? It was like having a word poised on the tip of the tongue and not being able to spit it out.

She and her husband hurried to the first-class carriage at the head of the train. I followed the green hat as it forged a path through the crowd. When they got to the carriage the man solicitously took her arm to assist her up but before she took that last step onto the train, she hesitated, turned and glanced again in my direction.

The train shunted back onto the main line. A warning whistle shrilled, followed by a general scramble as the passengers who were strolling about on the platform, hurried back. The conductor waited, green flag poised. He dropped his arm and the train heaved and jerked. The string of carriages lumbered forward, then jolted back on each other like an unco-ordinated caterpillar. Finally we eased out of the station and gathered speed.

My carriage was near the tail section and I could see the engine and front carriages snaking around a curve. Preoccupied as I was, I hardly noticed the steepled churches and big houses which streamed past the smoke-blackened windows.

It was a hot summer's day and the train racketing and swaying along the tracks to Pretoria was crowded with students on their way home for the holidays. We left the city behind, passing twisted tree trunks ripped by lightning and covered with weeds, then sped along miles of open *veld* before the bottles, rusted skeletons of old cars and smouldering rubbish heralded the arrival of yet another township.

At Irene where the train stopped for fifteen minutes, passengers leaned out of their windows to fling fruit and sandwiches to children who were begging alongside the tracks. I remained comfortably seated beside the window, nodding off in the sun.

I heard the quiet knock and thought that I had imagined it. It came again, louder this time. A little irritated at being disturbed, I got up to open the door. To my astonishment, standing in the doorway was the woman in green.

'Alice, thank goodness, I found you,' she said, slipping by me. Astounded, I automatically slid the door shut behind her.

'Henny Marais,' I gasped.

'*Ja*. It's me,' she laughed.

That laugh. How could I have forgotten? 'Henrika Marais,' I said again. 'I thought there was something familiar about you. It's been driving me mad,' I stepped back to get a better look at her. 'My God, you've changed so much.' No wonder I couldn't make the connection. 'What a surprise,' I cried, hugging her. 'It's been years ... years.'

'Twenty-five years,' she added.

'Sit down.' I patted the seat beside me.

'Listen Alice. I can't stay long. I'd love nothing better than to catch up with all the news, but I've got to get back to my husband.' She pulled a wry face and sat down anyway.

'For heaven's sake. What's the rush?'

'Are you still in Pretoria?' she asked.

I nodded.

'Alice I really can't stay,' she said. 'Give me your phone number, I'll get in touch with you when we get to Pretoria.'

I was still astonished at meeting her so unexpectedly. Then I remembered the white man with her and it all became crystal clear.

'I recognised you the moment I saw you at Park Station, but I couldn't come over.' She sensed that I had guessed the truth.

'I see.' I nodded slowly.

'Look, don't judge me until you've heard the whole story.'

She had tiny flecks of hazel in the grey of her irises. I remembered them from the time when we were little girls growing up in the Bazaar which was the colloquial term for the township then. 'It's not up to me to judge you.' I dropped my glance before replying.

'We'll catch up on everything. How about tomorrow? Are you busy?'

I shook my head.

'I'd better get going or my husband might come looking for me. Give me your phone number. I'll ring you in the morning.'

I rummaged through my handbag for a scrap of paper. All I could find was my cheque book. I ripped off the corner of a blank cheque and scribbled my name, address and phone number. 'Where's home now, Henny?' I asked.

'Kroonstad,' she said.

'Good Lord, don't tell me you're living in the Free State?'

'*Ja*. I married an Afrikaner.'

'I see,' I muttered.

'I thought that might surprise you. I am the wife of Deputy Minister Johan Mulder.'

I glanced at her in disbelief.

She nodded. 'We've been married for nineteen years ... and they've been the happiest years of my life,' she added. 'I have two grown sons.'

I was still incredulous.

'My past is dead, Alice. No one knows, not even Johan.'

'I see,' I muttered. 'I thought you had gone overseas.'

She raised a delicate shoulder. With the movement, the cameo caught my eye. I remembered now that it had once belonged to her mother. As a young girl I was always admiring and coveting it. Her mother used to tease me saying that one day when she was dead, I could have it.

'For how long will you be staying in Pretoria?' I asked.

'A week or so. My husband is here for a briefing before Parliament closes for the holidays.'

She got up to go. We hugged, promising to get together the next day. I let her out and locked the door behind her.

The train lurched and started to move out of Irene. The African children shouted, waving and running alongside the train. A sandwich flew by the window. The wax wrapping opened, spilling its contents into the dust. The children scrambled after it. A half-eaten apple followed the path of the sandwich.

The warmth and the rhythmic sway of the train soon dispelled all thoughts, including those of Henny, lulling me to sleep. I dreamed I was a child again, spending a Sunday morning at the zoo with my parents. We were walking along the shaded pathways towards the ravine where the big cats were housed. My father held my hand as we started out, but when we got to the ravine a stranger had taken his place.

I cried out for Daddy, thrashing and kicking, but the man lifted me over his shoulder like a sack of potatoes and carried me towards the ravine. I was still screaming for my father as I flew through the air into the lion's enclosure. Before I hit the ground, I awakened with a jolt. My heart pounding, I sat bolt upright and covered my face. It all came back to me. The woman in green and everything.

I sat up gathering my scattered wits and gazed out of the window, marvelling at how easily a dream is able to turn into a nightmare. A grove of pepper trees flashed by and in the distance the *Voortrekker* monument came into view.

We had almost arrived and I collected my belongings. I thought it best under the circumstances to delay disembarking in order to avoid Henny and the possibility of embarrassing her. I waited until most of the passengers had left the front carriages and then got off.

Amidst the noise and commotion I heard a page for Mr Mulder. He was a tall man and I saw his head moving towards the information booth. There was something very possessive in the way he held Henny's elbow and ushered her toward the rotunda. She saw me and gave a small nervous smile. I smiled back at her and walked by.

When I got home I told Aunty Dorothy about my unexpected encounter with Henny.

'What a coincidence,' Aunty Dorothy cried. 'Cousin Betty was telling me the other day that she had met her father, Piet Dimbaza, in O.K. Bazaars.'

'You're joking!'

'No. Cousin Betty said he came right up to her, tapped her on the shoulder and said, "Do you remember me Ousies". She said she almost died of fright. Then she recognised him. She says he's still a striking man. He told her he was living in Mamelodi and that he had a nice job in some government office.'

I listened in silence.

'What does she look like? I mean her hair … her father's a little backward in that respect. I was trying to remember what she was like as a child but I've forgotten.'

'She's the image of her mother.'

'What about her hair?'

'It's not as wild as it used to be. It's dark brown, it's not *kroes* just curly. Lots of curls like a perm I would say. When I saw her she had it tied back.'

'Good thing she didn't get his hair,' Aunty Dorothy said.

'She's got some of her father's looks. He was quite good-looking, but she definitely has her mother's eyes. They're grey with little flecks in them.'

'Oh, I remember now,' Aunty Dorothy said. 'What's her husband like?' she asked, settling down with her cup of tea, relishing the opportunity for a good bit of gossip.

'I didn't really get a good look at him, but from the little I saw, I think he's difficult and very possessive about her. He could be a real hard case. Oh yes, I almost forgot the most important bit. Do you know who he is?' I asked.

She shook her head, her eyes glinting eagerly.

'Johan Mulder.'

She stared back blankly.

'Deputy Minister Johan Mulder,' I said.

Aunty Dorothy's eyes opened wide. 'You mean … ?' she breathed.

168

Aunty Dorothy wanted to know every little detail. I told her all that I knew.

'Better not say anything to anyone,' I urged her when she left.

'Don't worry.' The look in her eyes, however, left me sceptical about this assurance.

'Whatever you do, stay away from Mrs Simons, you know what she's like, the old *skinderbek*.'

'Stop worrying about it, I know when to open my mouth and when to keep it shut,' she said.

When I looked out an hour later, I saw Aunty Dorothy heading down the road in the general direction of Mrs Simons, and I knew by the end of the day it would be all over the township.

Henny rang around noon. We talked on the phone for a while and I offered to pick her up the following day.

'Are you sure it won't be any trouble?' she asked.

'No trouble at all,' I replied.

'Okay I'll meet you in the lobby of my hotel.' She gave me the name and the address.

'Do you know where it is?' she asked.

'Yes I drive by there quite often.'

The hotel was a small, unpretentious but chic establishment near the university campus. I had no trouble finding her, even in the dimly lit lobby. She was the type of woman who stood out in any crowd. She was wearing a print dress, simple but elegant, with low-heeled pumps. Her hair was drawn back into a bun. It occurred to me then that she didn't look at all like a typical Afrikaner woman. It seemed incongruous that she could have buried herself in the heart of Afrikanerdom. I suspected that a woman like her would be painfully conspicuous and out of place in a right-wing Afrikaner community like Kroonstad. She had a straw hat in her hand and hurried over the moment she saw me.

'My car is outside.' I pointed to the slightly beaten-up Volkswagen across the street.

'Oh, good.' She dropped the sunglasses over her eyes. 'I was wondering whether you'd have transportation.'

'I call her "Old Faithful"; she hasn't let me down yet.' I laughed as we hurried across the street at the crossing.

I opened the door and threw some of the clutter onto the back seat. 'When were you last in Pretoria?' I asked.

'Not since I left here and went to Boxburg.'

'Not once?'

She shook her head. And when she saw my expression of surprise she said, 'When you hear the whole story, you'll understand.'

I started the car and we eased into the traffic. The jacaranda trees were in full bloom and it was truly a sight to behold. This was one time of the year when the city was exquisitely beautiful. The avenues of trees and the manicured gardens gave it an atmosphere of elegance that made one forget the harsh ugliness of the townships located miles out of the city. We passed the university campus and then took the road which passed by the zoo. I recalled the nightmare I had had on the train.

'Remember the zoo?' I asked.

'I was just thinking how much Nicholas and Ben would enjoy it.'

'Your children?'

She nodded. 'Nicholas has just turned eighteen and will be attending Stellenbosch University. My youngest is Ben. He's fourteen and he's at school in Bloemfontein.'

I listened as she talked about her boys.

'What about you?' she asked suddenly.

'I don't have any children. I was married for four years. David, my husband, was killed in a car accident. We'd postponed having children because of our careers. He was a doctor and I had just started teaching.' I hurried through this explanation not wanting to dwell on it.

'I'm sorry,' she said.

I shrugged. 'That's life.'

'You never got married again?'

170

'No.'

She stared out of the window in silence as we headed for the Bazaar. I saw her face reflected in the window, bright and alert with anticipation. At the corner where the Indian market used to be, I turned left. I still remember the distinctive morning smells of boiled mealies and peanuts, or frying meat.

'The market used to be here!' She was surprised that it wasn't where she had expected to find it. 'What happened to it?' she asked.

But before I could respond, it dawned on her. 'How stupid of me, I forgot everyone was moved out years ago.'

I slowed to a crawl and she looked about eagerly, trying to identify landmarks. Ahead of us the Imperial Bioscope rose from amidst the ruins like a shrine.

'It's hard to believe that it's all gone.'

'People were dispersed – the Indians to Laudium and the Coloureds to Eersterust.' We bumped over potholes and past a few remaining stores in the main street. 'They'll be moving those too,' I added.

We turned around in a large field. 'Our school used to be there ... and right here where we're parked is where Moosa's Cafe used to be. Remember the mango *achar* and thick slices of bread?'

'What happened to Moosa?'

'The old man died soon after they tore his shop down.'

I turned back into the main street. 'This is Third Street.' I turned into an empty lot overgrown with grass and weeds. 'This is about where your house used to be.'

'It was further down,' she argued.

'No. That's where the Pillays lived.'

'Of course, the Pillays and their ten children. I used to be beaten up regularly by the three older girls.'

'Because they thought you were Miss High-and-Mighty,' I reminded her.

'That wasn't true though.' She denied this with an expression of such serious indignation that it brought a smile to my face. 'I was shy, but not high and mighty.'

171

'You were okay,' I replied. She had always been quiet and aloof, almost stand-offish. The other children had mistaken this aloofness for weakness and had nicknamed her 'Mousy'. I always thought that her quietness had to do with the fact that her mother was white and her father black. They had got married in the early forties, long before laws were introduced prohibiting interracial marriages. Rumour had it then that her mother had fallen in love with him when he was still working on the farm for them as a labourer. He was a good-looking man who looked more coloured than African.

'I heard that after your mother died, you went to live in Boxburg with her sister. Your father just disappeared from the scene after Aunty Sophie died. Have you ever heard from him?'

'No.' She shook her head. 'The last I heard was that he was living with a black woman in one of the townships. But that was twenty years ago. He may be dead now for all I know.'

I didn't say anything. This was not the time to tell her that her father was alive and living in Mamelodi. I turned the car and we headed out of the Bazaar, past Mohammed's Furniture Emporium and A.B. Bazaars. 'I've arranged for us to have lunch at my place,' I said.

'That would be lovely. But are you sure I'm not putting you out?'

'Definitely not,' I assured her. 'My Aunty Dorothy prepared lunch. Remember her?'

She shook her head.

'She's a nurse. Actually a matron at the hospital now. She's a bright and efficient lady who has travelled all over. In fact she's just come back from Australia.' I went on and on about Aunty Dorothy. I wanted her to shine forth. I wanted desperately for Henny to see that we, too, had done something with our lives. We had not stagnated despite adversity.

The pale sky shimmered through a veil of heat. I rolled down the window and a blast of air caught her hat. I rolled the window up again.

'I'll take this off,' she said, placing her straw hat on the seat beside her.

172

'Aren't you going to tell me about your family? What happened after you left for Boxburg?'

She had lapsed into a comfortable silence and I waited impatiently to hear the rest of her story. Finally she said: 'Living with my white family, I became white. I went to a white school in Boxburg. It wasn't difficult. My mother had registered me as white on my birth certificate.'

The practice of having children from mixed marriages registered under the name and race of the white parent was a fairly common one.

'I did well at school, passed my matric and went to the University of Stellenbosch on a scholarship. I met Johan in my first year there. We got married and that was the end of my studies.'

There was a strange note in her voice and I couldn't quite decide whether it was regret or not. She lapsed again into a contemplative silence.

'That's it?' I asked.

'That's it.'

'Does your husband know ... ?'

'Of course not.' She shook her head emphatically. 'At times I've wanted to tell him, but how could I? If anyone ever found out that I had been fathered by a black man, his career and everything I hold dear would be destroyed; my marriage, my children.' She stared straight ahead, her face pale and pinched.

'Perhaps he loves you enough to accept it?' I suggested. 'Think of the peace of mind you'll have if it's all out in the open.'

'The scandal would destroy him.'

We stared at the road in silence. What a mess, I thought. Her worst nightmare would be being recognised by one of her old school friends while accompanying her husband. It wasn't that improbable, after all I had recognised her ... well, in a way, I conceded.

At Derdepoort the traffic increased. Most of the vehicles were loaded to the hilt with passengers. 'Pirate taxis from

173

Mamelodi,' I explained.

She chuckled. 'I remember how they used to pack people in, some of us sitting on the laps of others – complete strangers.'

'*Ja* and when the police were spotted, we all had to duck,' I laughed.

'Beneath the surface things haven't changed much, have they?'

I shook my head.

'The only difference is that we've grown older,' she added.

We passed a service station and turned left at the next intersection into Eersterust. It was a barren dusty township with rows of houses all having the same basic design. 'So this is Eersterust.' She looked around. 'I often think back to my childhood and the good times we had growing up. Life was quite different for me in Boxburg. Auntie was determined to turn me into a lady,' she smiled wryly. 'Johan believes that I was orphaned. I actually began to believe that myself. Do you know what I mean?'

I nodded. 'It's partly true anyway,' I remarked.

She glanced at me and then looked away, not quite sure what to make of my comment.

We stopped at a store to buy milk, then went home.

Home was two rooms in Aunty Dorothy's backyard. I had fixed them up as best I could, turning them into a comfortable little bed-sitter.

Aunty Dorothy had set the table and a small casserole stood on the warmer above the stove. There was a note from her to say that she hoped I didn't mind her coming in and doing a few things for me.

After lunch Henny and I looked through my old photograph album. We laughed and reminisced about old times. We argued a bit about politics, but nothing serious.

'Johan and I try not to discuss politics at home,' she said.

I wondered about her husband, wondered what sort of man he actually was. Somehow from what she said, I sensed a gap between them that had nothing to do with love, but more with a difference in perspective. She seemed almost intimidated by him.

She glanced at her watch.

'I'd like you to meet my aunty,' I said.

A look of alarm crossed her face.

'It'll only take a moment. I told her about you.'

'Okay,' she agreed.

'I would never have recognised you,' Aunty Dorothy said to Henny. 'Except your hair, maybe. I remember how wild it used to be when you were a child. Your mother used to sit out on the *stoep* combing your hair, and we could tell when this was happening because of your crying and screaming. *Ooh hene*, it was terrible. Your hair was so thick, it used to be a real paradise for lice,' she laughed. 'Now look how beautiful it is. My goodness. Come sit down here by me.' Aunty Dorothy patted the chesterfield beside her. She was a big woman and getting in and out of a chair was no easy task.

We stayed for quite a while and Aunty Dorothy told her all about her father.

She asked many questions and in the end she asked me: 'Did you know about this?'

'*Ja*, but I thought it would be best for Aunty Dorothy to tell you.'

'Aunty Dorothy, thank you,' she said gravely. 'I'm glad you told me.'

Eventually Henny caught my eye. I could see that she was anxious to get back.

'Are you ready to go back?' I asked.

She nodded. 'It's getting late. Johan will be wondering what's happened to me.'

Aunty Dorothy nodded.

'I'll get my keys.' I hurried to my own quarters.

When I got back the two women were waiting for me at the car.

'Goodbye Henny,' said Aunty Dorothy. 'I hope that things work out for you.'

Henny stepped forward and hugged Aunty Dorothy. I could see a tear gathering in the corner of Henny's eye. On the way back to the hotel, she was quiet.

'So now you know about your father,' I said.

We drove most of the way back in silence, except for the odd comment she made about something that caught her attention.

'How would you like to come to a *braaivleis* at the week-end?' she asked as I pulled up in front of her hotel.

'I don't think so.'

'I wish you'd come. It's at a Professor Malherbe's home. I'd like you to meet my husband.'

I shook my head. 'I don't think that's such a good idea, Henny.'

'Why not? You're a friend of mine.'

'Don't you think my presence would require awkward explanations?'

'Nonsense. Besides you don't look much different from any of them. Remember how we sometimes used to pass ourselves off as sisters?'

'You want me to play white,' I said bluntly.

'No. I just want you to come with me and be yourself.'

'Henny, please.'

'I need your support Alice. I need a friend.'

'You must have lots of friends.'

'Will you stop arguing,' she cried.

I laughed. It was all so outrageous.

'If you change your mind, let me know. Here's my number. The *braaivleis* is on Saturday.'

'You'll be going with your husband anyway,' I said.

'No I won't. He has a Saturday meeting. He'll meet me there of course, but much later in the afternoon.'

'Don't you know anyone there?'

'No.'

'What about this professor?'

'Never heard of him. The invitation is really for Johan, I'm just baggage,' she said dryly. 'I make a point of not

176

accompanying him on business trips. This has been the one exception.'

I thought of her often in the days that followed, and on Saturday afternoon I met her at her hotel.

'I'm so glad you decided to come,' she told me.

'I won't stay long. I just want to see how the other half lives,' I teased her. 'Your husband will be joining you anyway.'

The sprawling Malherbe home was located against the side of the mountain in a very select area, and from the driveway one could see all the way down to the manicured grounds of the Union Buildings.

There were at least a dozen cars parked in the driveway. I eased the Volkswagen in between a Lincoln Continental and a Mercedes.

We got out. I felt very awkward. She seemed oblivious to my discomfort. When we got to the door she hesitated, glanced at her reflection in the glass panel beside the door, and adjusted her hair.

I fumbled in my bag, patting for my purse and keys to make sure that they were all there, and looked about uneasily while Henny placed her finger on the doorbell. I could hear it echoing through the house.

We waited, but there was no answer.

'Let's go around the side.'

We heard the sound of splashing water and loud laughter and came upon a group of golden-limbed sun-worshippers splayed in wide-legged ecstasy around the brilliant aquamarine of the pool.

I hesitated for a moment, intimidated by the large crowd. Henny stood looking around trying to find a familiar face.

'Yoo! hoo!' Someone waved and called.

I directed Henny's attention to the far end of the terrace.

'Oh, there's Rebecca.' Her face lit up. 'She's Johan's secretary.'

'You told me that you didn't know anyone here,' I reproached her.

'Oh, come on,' she said gaily. 'I'm glad she's here. She's very nice. You'll like her.' Henny briskly started out to where a woman sat cross-legged on the grass amidst the purple blossoms shed by the Grandaddy of Jacaranda trees, its branches so gnarled and overgrown that it covered most of the terrace.

It was late afternoon and sizzling on the spit for the evening's *braaivlies* was the carcass of a lamb. The delicious aroma of scorched meat wafted on the air. I walked by the spit, glancing at the carcass slowly and lusciously rotating over the coals. The servant in a stiffly-starched, white jacket was basting the lamb. I slowed down and arranged a smile on my face for his benefit. Somehow I felt like a fellow conspirator. Neither of us belonged.

I lagged behind and Henny waited for me. We joined Rebecca. 'I suppose Johan is still in a meeting. My God, you look fresh,' she remarked dabbing at her brow with a handkerchief.

'I'm so glad you're here,' Henny said to Rebecca and then introduced me. For a moment attention was focused on me and I nodded and muttered my acknowledgement, wishing that I were somewhere other than here.

Fortunately the conversation revolved around Henny. Questions were asked about her husband and I had a chance to collect my thoughts.

'What are you doing tomorrow?' Rebecca demanded, including me in her smile.

I had been introduced as a friend and so far there had been no awkward questions.

'She might have other plans,' Rebecca's husband interrupted.

'Of course. I'm sorry if I appear forward. My weakness you know,' Rebecca laughed.

I smiled distractedly.

'Sit down here,' Rebecca said. We squatted in the shade of the tree, and were soon joined by others.

I was hot and uncomfortable and edged away, finding a spot on the grass against the trunk of the tree.

'Something wrong?' Rebecca called.

I shook my head. 'I'll be all right in a minute.'

I must have dozed off for I awakened to the sound of voices raised in argument. I sat up with a start and realised that there was a heated discussion going on. I leaned back against the tree trunk, reflecting that people weren't all that different. The same thing happened whenever we got together at a picnic too. I listened to parts of the conversation, my mind drifting around aimlessly.

'Give them the franchise and we'll drown in a sea of black vengeance. You mark my words,' a freckle-faced young man said adjusting his glasses and glaring at the faces around him.

I wondered what these self-righteous people would say if they knew that I was an interloper.

'It'd be a lot better for us to sit back and let them kill each other off,' the freckle-faced youth continued. 'I am a second generation Rhodesian and look what happened to us. On the other hand we could wait until the country falls apart. When it's in a shambles they'll be begging us to recolonise them.'

'Don't hold your breath,' someone chipped in dryly.

'Oh God, not another social history of the colonial inferiority complex,' groaned one of the girls who had just come out of the pool, as she bent forward and towelled her long blonde hair.

There was a sprinkling of derisive laughter.

'You're just a bunch of hypocrites,' the girl said, tossing her long mane like a colt and striding back to the pool. Then turning to scowl at them she stepped onto the diving-board. Her body arched like that of a graceful dancer while she stood poised on the edge. Then, aware of the interest in her, she jack-knifed, cleanly cutting through the water.

'Nice dive,' someone called.

'Could've been an Olympic hopeful if we hadn't been kicked out of the bloody Olympics,' said a fellow who was built like a rugby player.

'I think the whole bloody world's gone crazy,' one of the girls of the flat-chest-firm-thigh variety added, leaping to her

179

feet. She was a pretty girl, about twenty, darkly tanned with dark hair and brown eyes. 'You'd think that other countries would have their hands too full with their own problems to still worry about us.'

There was a surprised pause and all eyes turned to her.

'What more do they want us to do? In this country the Blacks live well; they have the highest standard of living in Africa,' she continued, her face red with indignation. 'I think it's just a small bunch of communists going around making trouble. I say keep them in their place. I don't want to mix with Blacks and I sure as hell don't want to marry one of them. I'm proud that I don't have any black blood in me.'

Her outburst was followed by a startled silence.

'But my dear we all have,' Henny said sarcastically.

'Not me. My ancestors are all direct descendants of the *voortrekkers*,' she snapped with comic pique.

A baby-faced boy laughed. 'They were the worst offenders.'

'You bloody liberals have screwed up our country,' someone complained.

'Things are going from bad to worse. Few of us sleep soundly at night any more. My father sleeps with a revolver under his pillow,' the freckle-faced youth added.

I enjoyed a good vantage point and I could see their expressions. I was watching Henny. Her lip curled contemptuously, her eyes like flints of steel. The argument continued but I wasn't listening any more. The words merely splashed against my consciousness.

Henny got to her feet, picked up her hat and inclined her head towards me. I got up too, dusting the grass from my dress.

'I think it's time for me to go,' she said. 'I'll give you a call,' she told Rebecca, who watched her in dismay.

'You've just got here,' she complained. 'Aren't you waiting for Johan?'

'Please tell him that I've returned to the hotel.'

'God, I couldn't stand any more of that,' she groaned as we got into the car. 'I'm not in the mood for it. You know what I'd really like to do?' she asked.

'What?'

'I'd like to see my father.'

I didn't say anything, merely concentrated on the road back to the hotel, thinking about the conversation and wondering how she was going to get hold of her father. I sensed that something was going to happen. I left her at the hotel with a feeling of disquiet. Something was going to happen. I could sense the tension, like the building up of a storm.

I waited all the next day for her to call, and when she didn't, I started worrying about her. Finally I gathered my courage and telephoned. Her husband answered the phone and said that she wasn't in. From his aloof tone I suspected that there was a problem. I asked him to give her a message, but she never called. That was it. I never heard a word about her again. Occasionally her husband was mentioned in a news report; once I even thought of phoning her, but changed my mind, reluctant about intruding. If she wanted to get hold of me, she had my number, I reasoned.

Two years later, I was walking down the main street with Aunty Dorothy when a man stopped us with a: '*My hene is dit jy Dorothy?*'

Aunty Dorothy came to an abrupt halt and gave the man one of her 'looks'. Then her expression softened with recognition. She looked quite taken aback as the man grasped her hand, shaking it energetically. 'I would never have recognised you,' she cried, and turning to me said: 'Alice, remember *Oom* Piet ... Henny's father?'

There were the usual exchanges. I told him that I had met Henny two years ago, and described some of the circumstances of this meeting.

'*Ja*, I saw her too. She telephoned me and came to see me. I was so surprised, but my heart was really glad that she hadn't forgotten me altogether.' He shook his head as if he still could not believe it.

181

'I didn't see her again after the *braaivleis* at Professor Malherbe's house. I waited and waited for her to call, but I think there was some trouble with her husband,' I said.

He shook his head sadly.

'*Ja*, I know. She told me.' He glanced away.

'Where is she now?' I asked.

'Don't you know?' he asked, surprised.

'No.'

'She's dead.'

'What!' I gasped.

He nodded. 'I got a card from her husband. She went off her head and died in the asylum.'

'I didn't read anything about it in the papers,' I said, still shocked by the news.

'You know how these white people are, *mos*. If they want you to know they tell you, if they don't they keep it quiet,' *Oom* Piet said. 'She had a nervous breakdown or something.' He shook his head, sighed, and kicked the toe of his shoe against the pavement.

I could see in that gesture a lifetime of regret.

'Too bad things didn't turn out for her,' he continued.

'What about her husband?' I asked.

'He married again. I read something about *that* in the newspaper,' he said.

Aunty Dorothy gave me a rueful smile.

'Anyway, I got to go,' he said. 'Maybe one of these days I'll visit you. I know where you are in Eersterust.'

'*Ja*, okay,' Aunty Dorothy said.

I mumbled a goodbye and watched the old man crossing the street, expertly weaving his way through the traffic.

GLOSSARY

achar   chutney

ag   oh, so

amandla   power (Zulu), used politically as a cry for black freedom

baas   boss

bobbejaan   monkey

bonsella   gift

boer (pl. boere)   originally farmer, Afrikaans-speaking whites (slang)

boet   brother

boetie   brother (dim.)

braaivleis   barbecue

bredie   casserole

buti   brother

champals   sandals, thongs

chorrie   old wreck

coolie

dagga   cannabis

doek   cloth often used as headscarf

dom kop   fool

donder   (lit. thunder), to beat up, bugger (slang)

dorp   village

driehoek   triangle

ghee   clarified butter

hene   goodness!

hotnot   Hottentot (abbrev.), term used by whites for Khoi-Khoi, original settlers in Cape area, and today for coloured people (pej.)

iGoldie   Golden City (colloq.)

iNigilani   England

jong   chap, fellow (slang)

jou   you

kaffir meid   black maid

kaloko   by the way (Xhosa, colloq.)

karoo semi-desert region
kerel fellow
kierie walking stick
klein missies little miss
knobkierie fighting stick
kopje hill
kraal enclosed village
kroeskop, kroes crinkly, eg hair
lambele hungry
leguan large lizard like an iguaga
maak gou hurry up!
magou liquid from maize-meal porridge which is drunk
   (Tswaṇa)
marshallah exclamation using the name of Allah
mealies, mealie-meal maize
misies madam, form of address to employer, woman
   in charge
molo, buti good morning, brother
mos of course
My hene is dit jy? My goodness is that you?
nasie nation
ne an interrogative
nou ja now then
oom uncle
oompie uncle (dim.)
ouma grandmother
oupa grandfather
outa elderly black person
pondokkies shanties
pasop beware
roti unleavened bread
shebeen illegal drinking hall
siesie sister (Xhosa), term of endearment
sjambok whip
skinderbek gossip-monger
skollies petty criminal, hooligan (Cape, colloq.)
stadig steady, slow

stoep   verandah
tante   aunt
tata   father
Thixo   God
tog   so
tou   rope
tsak   bugger off!
tsotsi   township hooligan, petty criminal
umfaan   young man
utywala   African beer
veld   open country
veldskoen   shoe, hand-made (usually by Boers) of cured
   ox-leather
verdomde   damned
voortrekker   Afrikaner settler
vreugde   pleasure
vrot   rotten
Wat het ons hier?   What have we here?
Wat soek jy?   What are you looking for?